27 Nov 2009

Dear Anisha.

Happy Reading !

love,

Ashwin

CLASSIC
Fairy TALES

CLASSIC
Fairy TALES

Retold and Illustrated by
Michael Foreman

STERLING
New York / London
www.sterlingpublishing.com

To our sons,
Jack, Ben and Mark.
For times had
and stories shared.

First published in Great Britain in 2005
by Pavilion Children's Books.

Library of Congress Cataloging-in-Publication Data Available

10 9 8 7 6 5 4

Published in 2005 by Sterling Publishing Co., Inc.
387 Park Avenue South, New York, NY 10016
© 2005 by Michael Foreman
Designed by Janet James
Distributed in Canada by Sterling Publishing
c/o Canadian Manda Group, 165 Dufferin Street
Toronto, Ontario, Canada M6K 3H6

Printed in China
All rights reserved

ISBN 978-1-4027-2865-5

For information about custom editions, special sales, premium and
corporate purchases, please contact Sterling Special Sales
Department at 800-805-5489 or specialsales@sterlingpub.com.

Contents

"To his amazement the thorns
turned to blossom…"

Sleeping BEAUTY

In a far away land a king and queen were sad because they had no children. Then, one day, the queen at last gave birth to a little daughter. The king was overjoyed and ordered a christening feast more splendid and spectacular than any seen before.

The king didn't want just ordinary godmothers for his precious little daughter. He wanted fairy godmothers and invited all twelve fairies who lived in his kingdom to the christening: hoping that each might bestow a special gift on the little princess.

After the christening all the guests proceeded to the great banqueting hall and, in front of each fairy godmother was placed a magnificent jewelled dish, and a knife, fork and spoon of pure gold.

But then, just as all the guests had sat down and the doors to the palace kitchens opened and servants appeared with the first great silver trays of delicious food, an old forgotten fairy arrived. She had not left her tower in a remote part of the kingdom for fifty years and people had thought she must be dead.

The king ordered a place to be set for her but, as he had only instructed the royal jeweler to make twelve jeweled dishes for the twelve invited fairies, the old fairy was given a dish of common earthenware. She was very upset and muttered angry threats which were overheard by one of the younger fairies sitting next to her.

The young fairy, alarmed by the threats to the baby, hid herself behind one of the tapestries in the hall. The fairies now offered their wishes to the baby princess, all of which were bound to come true.

The first wished that the princess would grow to be the most beautiful lady in the world; the second, that she would have the virtue of an angel; the third that she should sing like a nightingale, and so on with the others—everything that anyone would wish for.

Then it was the old fairy's turn. "Because you did not invite me, and because you gave me this old pot to eat from, my wish for the baby is that in her fifteenth year she shall prick her finger with a spindle and drop down dead."

Well, you can imagine the shock that this terrible wish caused. The queen began weeping and wailing and the king leapt to his feet in anger, but the old fairy had vanished. Now the whole christening party was in anguish.

Then, the young fairy stepped out from the shadows. "I have saved my wish to the end, but I'm afraid it is not powerful enough to completely undo what the old fairy has done. The princess *will* prick her finger with a spindle, but she will *not* sink into the sleep of death, but into a sleep that will last for one hundred years."

The king, hoping to save his daughter, sent out his messengers to all corners of the land. "Burn all the spinning wheels!" he commanded. "Make sure all spindles are destroyed!"

And so the years rolled by and the princess grew up virtuous, clever and beautiful. Each of the wishes of the fairy godmothers was coming true, and the king and queen lived in fear that the dreaded wish of the old witch would also be fulfilled.

One day, the king, queen and princess visited one of their many castles in a remote corner of the land. While her parents attended to matters of state, the princess happily played with her little dog, Mop, playing 'hide and seek' around the great halls and galleries and followed winding stairs to the top of all the towers.

At the top of the very last tower, Mop sniffed interestedly at the door. "What have you found there, Mop?" asked the princess. She pushed at the door and it creaked open to reveal a very tiny room.

To the princess's great surprise, an old woman was sitting in the corner, her wizened hands working away with some thread and a

whirling wooden machine which the princess didn't recognize. "Good day to you, old lady," said the princess. "What are you doing?"

"I am spinning," replied the old lady who, working alone in the high tower, had never heard the king's order to destroy all spinning wheels.

"Oh, please my I try?" cried the princess, fascinated by the whirling wheel and flashing spindle. "I've never seen one before." Slowly, the old lady got to her feet and the princess took her place at the wheel. However, as soon as she touched the spindle, she pricked her finger and fell to the floor in a deep sleep.

The old lady screamed for help and Mop raced up and down the stairs, barking in alarm. Servants came running and sprinkled water on the princess, rubbed perfume onto her temples and slapped her hands. Mop licked his mistress's face but nothing, nothing, would wake her.

Then the king arrived, breathless and red in the face after hurrying up the winding stairway. He fell on his knees beside his daughter, beat his fists upon the floor, and cried out in anguish, "The dreadful prophecy has come true!"

He got to his feet when the queen arrived, and consoled his wife, then ordered that their beautiful daughter be taken to the finest room in the castle and there placed on a bed of pure white silk. Then he commanded that the good young fairy be sent for. "Perhaps there is still something she can do to bring our lovely girl back to us."

The swiftest courier in the land was a dwarf in super-fast seven league boots, and he was sent to find the young fairy who was far away in a distant country. The young fairy returned within hours in a flying chariot drawn by firey dragons.

She was taken immediately to the chamber where the princess lay on her silken bed, beautiful but deeply, deeply asleep.

"Yes," said the fairy after listening to the princess's slowly beating heart. "She will sleep for one hundred years but I will make sure she is not alone when she wakes."

Then, with the king's permission, she kissed the ring on her little finger and made a fairy wish. Immediately, the king and queen, the little dog Mop, the courtiers and page boys all fell into a deep, deep sleep. Servants, soldiers, cleaners scrubbing steps, cooks and kitchen boys, even the horses, ducks and chickens in the yard, froze in mid-movement and slipped into a slumber which would be undisturbed until the princess woke and needed them again. Spiders, in the deepest darkest corners, could not even cover the castle and all the sleeping inhabitants in a gigantic web, because they, too, were fast asleep.

The pigeons on the roofs tucked their heads under their wings and slumbered, as did the swifts and swallows in their nests clinging to the turrets and battlements. Even the very flames in the great fireplaces died down and slept, waiting to be rekindled in the twinkling of a princess's eye.

Within an hour there sprang up around the castle a forest so thick with thorns that no man nor beast could pass through. Only the top of the highest tower could be seen above the dense and towering trees. During the long years that followed many brave knights and princes tried to force their way through to the castle but all became hopelessly entangled and died in the grip of the thorn forest.

Then, one day, a prince out hunting saw the tower above the forest and asked who lived there. Some said the castle was the home of ogres, or witches, others spoke of giants and evil spirits. The prince did not know who to believe, until one old man told him a story his grandfather had heard from *his* grandfather.

"My Lord, the story goes that the most beautiful princess in the whole world sleeps in that castle. They say it is a sleep of one hundred years, until the prince who is meant to be hers, comes to wake her."

The prince was hugely excited. This was the story he wished to believe, and no threat of ogres, witches, giants or the like would dissuade him. He leapt from his horse, drew his sword, and began to cut his way through the forest of thorns.

To his amazement the thorns turned to blossoms before the swish of his sword, and parted to let him through, then turned to thorns and closed behind him again.

He pushed on, deeper and deeper into the forest which flowered before him and closed thick and thorny behind.

When the prince came at last to the castle he passed by guards like snoring statues and entered the main courtyard where horses slumbered in their stables and stable boys stood stock still with buckets and brooms. He stepped around kneeling cleaning ladies in mid-scrub, and climbed the wide marble stairway into the great hall where slept the king and queen and all the members of the royal court.

"What strange magic is this?" wondered the prince. "What deep spell covers this castle at the heart of the enchanted forest?"

But soon it was the heart of the prince which became enchanted when he at last came upon the princess asleep on her bed of pure white silk. He was spellbound by her beauty, and for a few moments stood as still as every other thing in the castle. The only movements came from the tiny specks of dust in the sunbeams which shone through the window and seemed to bathe the sleeping princess in a shower of shimmering diamonds.

Then the prince bent down and kissed her forehead. He felt an eyelash brush his cheek and as he drew back to look at her, the

princess awoke. Sunbeams and diamonds were as nothing compared to the eyes of the princess. And as for her, she only had eyes for her prince.

In that instant the castle came alive again around them. King, queen and courtiers yawned and stretched, fires flamed once more beneath bubbling pots and cauldrons; cooks shouted at kitchen boys, horses stamped, stable boys set to with buckets and brooms and the guards snapped to attention and winked at the servant girls for the first time in a hundred years. Pigeons cooed and spiralled into the blue sky and swifts and swallows swooped around the castle towers.

A year and a day later the princess married her prince and they
made the castle in the forest their home. It was now a castle full of
life and joy, in a forest of blossom and butterflies, with far more roses
than thorns.

"...take Queeny Cream to market and
sell her. Be sure you get a good price."

Jack
AND THE
Beanstalk

Long ago, a poor widow lived in a little cottage with her only son, Jack. They had no furniture except one wooden stool and a rickety table, so Jack and his mother had to sleep on the floor. They had a cow called Queeny Cream who gave them milk every morning, which they carried to market and sold. This was all they had to live on and times were very hard.

Then, one morning, Queeny Cream produced no milk. Then the next day, no milk, and the day after and the day after that, no milk. A whole week went by with no milk and, therefore, no money for food.

The poor widow saw that the only way to save herself and her little son from starving was to sell the cow. "I'm too weak to go myself, Jack, so you must take Queeny Cream to market and sell her. Be sure you get a good price."

Jack felt quite important as he strode along the country road leading Queeny Cream by her halter. He enjoyed going to market, it was a beautiful day, and he felt quite the young businessman.

He hadn't gone very far before he met an old man wearing a tall crown hat. "Good morning, Jack me lad," said the old man, "and where are you off to?"

"Good morning to you, sir," said Jack, wondering how the old man knew his name. "I'm going to market to sell our cow."

"Oh, you don't need to take the poor creature all that way," said the old man. "She looks worn out already. I'll buy her from you here and now. What's more, I'll give you ten—I repeat, ten—of these magic beans for her!"

Jack looked at the beans in the old man's hand. They did look beautiful, red and shiny and speckled brown.

"Tell you what," said the old man seeing that Jack was unsure what to do, "to make it fair, let's do it this way." He began counting the beans into Jack's hand. "One for you, one for me. One more for you, one for me. One for you, one for me. One for you, one for me. Another one for you, and one for me. That's five each and I'll give you another one for luck. Now you've got more than me."

"So I have!" cried Jack and handed over the cow, convinced he had made a great bargain.

Jack whistled happily all the way home.

"Home already, Jack? said his mother. "That was quick. How much did you get for our cow?"

"All these!" said Jack, and laid the beans out on the rickety table.

"Beans!" cried his mother. "Beans! You sold Queeny Cream for a few beans? Why, there's not even enough here to make bean soup!" And she gathered up the beans and threw them out of the window. "No supper for you, my lad. Under the table with you, and go to sleep."

So, sad and hungry, Jack lay on the hard floor and tried to sleep. He was terribly upset because he had disappointed his mother so badly, and he was still confused by the trick the old man had played on him.

Next morning it was strangely dark in the little cottage. Instead of daylight shining through the window, Jack could see nothing but a dark green wall. He called to his mother and they both ran outside to see, hard against their home, a giant green beanstalk, fatter than the broadest oak, towering up and up into the clouds!

"The beans, the magic beans!" gasped Jack. "Oh mother," he said "they were magic," and he began to climb the beanstalk.

"Jack!" cried his mother, "what do you think you are doing? Where are you going?"

"To the top, to the top," and soon he was out of sight. There were so many huge leaves and shoots and tendrils that Jack found it an easy climb. The cottage and the fields he knew vanished beneath the

clouds and, when he reached the top of the beanstalk, it seemed like another world. The topmost branches were enormous and spread out across the clouds like lush meadows sprinkled with star-shaped flowers and, beside a lake shaped like a new moon stood a great castle. Jack, excited by the climb to this secret land in the sky, marched boldly up to the huge castle door.

To the side of the door hung a bell pull, but it was too high for Jack to reach. He jumped and jumped but couldn't reach it but, as luck would have it, the door suddenly creaked open and an enormous woman, a giantess with one eye in the middle of her forehead, glared down at him.

Jack turned to run but the giantess grabbed him by his heel and carried him, dangling upside down, into the castle kitchen. "Ho, ho, ho," she chortled, "you shall be my little helper. You shall clean and scrub and do as I say when my husband is out, and when he is home, I must hide you because he doesn't like children, except on toast."

Then, just as she set Jack to work on a great pile of greasy dishes, Thump! Thump! Thump! Thump! The whole castle began to shudder with the sound of someone coming. Someone big. Someone very, very, big.

"Oh no! It's my old man, home already," said the giantess. "Quick, hide. Hide in here." And she bundled Jack into a cupboard next to the oven. The keyhole was so big it admitted plenty of air and Jack could see everything that took place through it.

Jack knew giants were supposed to be big, but not that big!

The giant sniffed the air and then bellowed:

"Fe, Fi, Fo, Fum,

I smell the breath of a little one

Be he alive or be he dead,

I'll grind his bones to make my bread."

Ooooooh! How Jack trembled and how Jack shook, but he couldn't resist another look.

"There's someone in this castle and I want him for my dinner," bellowed the giant.

"No, no, dear," said his wife, "It's probably a few greasy scraps left from that boy you ate yesterday. Relax, put your feet up and I'll get your dinner ready in no time."

Soon the giant was wiping his chin after eating two boiled sheep and a dozen roast chickens. Then he went for a walk to build up his appetite for tea.

The giantess got Jack from the cupboard and set him to work with the dirty dishes and pots and pans. When they heard the giant returning, Jack was put back in the cupboard.

When the giant had finished his huge dinner, (three little pigs and a pair of swans) he ordered his wife to bring him his gold so that he might count it before supper time.

The giantess plonked six heavy sacks on the table and then went off to dig vegetables for her husband's supper. The giant began counting his gold pieces into bags and, by and by, he fell asleep amongst his gold. He began to snore like thunder.

Quietly, Jack crept out of the cupboard, picked up a big bag of gold and ran to the beanstalk. He dropped the bag down into the clouds and clambered down the stalk after it.

Jack's mother heard a great thump and rushed into her garden fearing Jack had fallen, but found a bag of gold had dropped out of the sky. Then Jack arrived, sliding down the last few feet of beanstalk and danced around the bag of gold. At last, they had something to celebrate!

Next day, when his mother went off to market with a gold piece in her pocket, Jack could not resist another climb up the beanstalk. But, this time, he dyed his hair black.

Again, just as he got to the castle door, the giantess grabbed him and carried him inside.

"I've just lost a boy like you. My husband must have gobbled him up when I wasn't looking," she said. "You can finish his work."

And she set him cleaning a mountain of greasy pots. Soon, the same terrifying sound came again. Thump! Thump! Thump!

"Quick! My old man's coming. Get into the cupboard and don't make a sound."

Ooooooh! How Jack trembled and how Jack shook as the giant bellowed out in his commanding voice:

"Fe, Fi, Fo, Fum!

I smell the breath of a little one.

Be he alive or be he dead,

I'll grind his bones to make my bread."

"No, no dear. Meatballs!" said the giantess. "You can smell the meatballs I'm boiling for you dinner. Sit down, it's almost ready."

When he had gobbled up the boiled meatballs and swallowed a bucket of ale, his wife brought him a little brown hen . . . alive and clucking.

Jack, peering through the keyhole, was horrified, fearing the giant would swallow the hen alive, feathers and all. But the giant stood the hen on the table and said, "Lay!" And she instantly laid a golden egg. "Lay!" said the giant again. And she laid another. "Lay!" he repeated a third time, and a third golden egg lay on the table. The giantess took the eggs away and, by and by, the giant fell asleep with his head on the table.

Quietly, quietly, Jack crept from the cupboard towards the snoring giant, picked up the little brown hen, ran out of the castle and climbed down the beanstalk as fast as he could go.

At first, Jack's mother was disappointed when, instead of a bag of gold, he handed her a little brown hen. But not when Jack said "Lay!" and out popped a golden egg! "Lay!" said Jack again, and there on the rickety table lay another golden egg.

Next day, when his mother went to market to order a nice new table, Jack thought he would make one more trip up the beanstalk. This time, he cut his hair really, really short, and again the one eyed giantess did not recognize him and dragged him into the castle and set him to work.

"My husband can't stop snacking on little boys," she said. "When he comes home we'll have to hide you somewhere special."

Thump! Thump! Thump!

"Oh dear, oh dear. It's my old man home early. Quick, in here." And the giantess pulled Jack out of the kitchen and into a room with a vast bed and popped him in a wardrobe.

"Fe, Fi, Fo, Fum!
I smell the breath of a little one.
Be he alive or be he dead,
I'll grind his bones to make my bread."

"No dear, it's your tasty dinner you can smell. You're home early but I'll have it ready on the table in no time."

"I've been looking all over for that little brown hen and I'm tired," the giant said. "I think I'll have a bit of a lie down before dinner." And he stomped through into the bedroom and collapsed onto the vast bed. Jack heard the bedsprings groaning under the giant's weight and then the sound of the most beautiful music he had ever heard filled the room.

Jack opened the wardrobe door very, very slightly and saw, in a corner of the room, a harp, made all of gold, playing itself. No one touched the strings but they moved as if breathed on by angels. The lovely music soon lulled the giant to sleep and when his snores were louder than the music, Jack crept from his hiding place, grabbed the golden harp and ran.

"Master! Master!" cried the harp and the giant woke up with a roar!

Ooooooh! How Jack trembled and how Jack shook, and over his shoulder he took one last look.

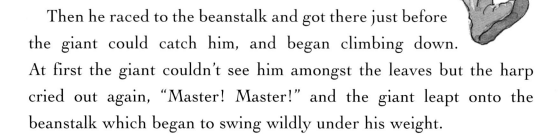

Then he raced to the beanstalk and got there just before the giant could catch him, and began climbing down. At first the giant couldn't see him amongst the leaves but the harp cried out again, "Master! Master!" and the giant leapt onto the beanstalk which began to swing wildly under his weight.

Jack slipped and slithered down the stalk as fast as he could with the harp under one arm and, when he got near the bottom, he yelled, "Mother! Mother! Get the axe!"

So his mother ran with an axe in her hand to the foot of the beanstalk and then screamed as she saw the giant coming out of the clouds. Jack tumbled to the ground, grabbed the axe and chop, chop, chopped until the beanstalk and the giant came crashing to earth.

When the dust had settled, Jack saw that their cottage lay flattened under the giant, who was quite dead.

"Oh dear, oh dear," cried his mother, "wherever shall we live now?"

"Never mind, Mother," replied Jack, "we have enough gold to build a palace." And the golden harp began to play, and Jack and his mother danced around the little brown hen who sat and clucked on a growing pile of golden eggs.

"Then she sat in the chimney corner and began to cry."

Cinderella

 There once lived a man who married twice and his second wife was the most stuck up and snooty woman in the world. She already had two daughters who were just as unpleasant as their mother.

The man's first wife had given him a daughter of his own before she died and she was a lovely and sweet-natured girl.

The new wife began to show how unkind she could be. She could not bear her stepdaughter's good qualities because it made her own daughters seem even worse than they were.

So she made her do all the hard work around the house. She had to wash all the windows, scrub the stairs, polish the floors, chop the wood, and cook and serve all the meals. Then do all the dishes. Her sisters didn't have to lift a finger. They sat about all day in their fine dresses and went to parties in the evening. However, they grew more ugly because their hearts were bitter, which made their faces sour.

The ugly sisters slept in soft feather beds in elegant rooms, while their poor sister slept on a hard, thin mattress in a tiny room at the top of the house.

The poor, sweet-natured girl just did the work and didn't complain to her father because she knew he was under the spell of his bossy wife. When her day's work was done, the girl was left to sit alone in the chimney corner, warming herself by the dying fire.

Seeing her sitting by the cinders in her shabby clothes, the rest of the family nicknamed her Cinderella. However, even in her dirty clothes, Cinderella was a hundred times more beautiful than her sisters.

One day wonderful new dresses were delivered to the house. There was going to be a grand ball at the palace and the sisters had been invited.

All the ugly sisters could talk about was what they would wear and what make-up they would use and which elaborate hairstyles to have. This meant even more work for Cinderella because she had to iron all their fine petticoats and starch their ruffles. It didn't occur to the her to ask, "What about me? Why can't I go to the ball?"

The ugly sisters asked her advice about everything because she had such good taste. She not only advised them well, but offered to dress their hair, which they were very willing to let her do.

They ate nothing but salad for two days and laced themselves tight to make their waists as slender as possible and squeezed into their gorgeous gowns. Cinderella did their hair and make-up for them, and helped them into their carriage and waved until they were out of sight. Then she sat in the chimney corner and began to cry.

A cat brushed against her leg and Cinderella said, "Oh puss, where did you come from? I am so unhappy," and the cat replied, "Meow," and, to Cinderella's surprise, in a flash of light turned into a little old woman. "Dearie me! Why all the tears, my child?" the old woman asked kindly.

"Oh, I wish..." sighed Cinderella.

"You wish to go to the ball, don't you?" said the little old woman.

"With all my heart," said Cinderella. "But how can I?"

"Well, let's see what we can do about that!" cried the old woman. "Now, do as I say. Go into the garden and pick a plump pumpkin."

Cinderella wondered how a pumpkin could help her get to the ball but she fetched the biggest pumpkin she could find. The old lady took the pumpkin and scooped out the inside, leaving nothing but the shell. Then, she touched it with her ring—and instantly the pumpkin changed into a golden coach, sparkling in the evening sunshine. Cinderella was amazed.

"Now," said the old lady, "go to the pantry and look in the mousetrap. Bring me what you find." Cinderella looked in the mousetrap and saw six mice which she took to the old lady who touched them with her ring.

Instantly they were transformed into six prancing mouse-colored horses with glossy manes and handsome long tails. They shook their manes and frisked their tails and seemed to bow towards Cinderella, who clapped her hands in delight.

"Now, we need a coachman," said the old woman briskly. "Bring me the rat trap."

By this time Cinderella could hardly believe what was going on.

She ran down to the cellar and brought up the rat trap in which were three fat rats. One of them had a fine set of whiskers, so the old woman chose that one; when she touched him with her ring he changed into a fat, jolly coachman in full uniform. Cinderella could hardly believe her eyes.

"We're not finished yet," said the old woman with a sparkle in her eyes. "Go into the garden. Behind the watering can you will find six lizards. Bring them to me."

Cinderella found the lizards which she put into her apron and brought to the old lady. Another touch of the ring changed them into six smart footmen who sprang onto the rear of the coach as if they had been doing it all their lives.

"There!" cried the old woman. "Now they will take you to the ball!"

"But how can I go like this?" asked Cinderella, looking down at the rags she had been doing housework in all day. "I won't be allowed in wearing these old clothes."

The old woman smiled and touched the hem of Cinderella's tattered apron with her walking stick. Cinderella felt a tingle all over her. She shut her eyes tightly and when she opened them again her ragged clothes had transformed into a magnificent silver and gold ball gown, decorated with precious rubies and blue lapis. And on Cinderella's feet were a pair of glass slippers, the prettiest in the whole world.

Two footmen opened the door and assisted the beautifully dressed, and rather astounded, Cinderella into the coach. Then the old woman warned Cinderella that on no account must she stay at the ball after the clock had struck twelve. "If you stop a single moment beyond that time, the fine coach, horses, coachman, footmen and your fine

clothes, will all turn back into a pumpkin, mice, rats, lizards and your old rags."

Cinderella promised to leave the ball before midnight and set off in her golden coach.

When she got to the palace the king's son was informed that a beautiful and unknown lady had arrived. The prince hurried to the door and welcomed Cinderella. He took her hand and led her into the grand ballroom where a great and glittering company was assembled.

As soon as they saw her, all conversation stopped; the people stopped dancing and the musicians stopped playing, so great was the effect of the stranger's beauty.

Cinderella was unnerved by the sudden silence as all eyes turned towards her. Then a murmur of admiration spread through the crowd: "How beautiful she is!"

Even the old king could not stop staring at her and remarked to the queen that he had not seen such a beauty for a long time.

The prince asked Cinderella for the pleasure of dancing with her, and the music started again. The prince danced with Cinderella until a magnificent feast was served. Cinderella sat near her sisters and chatted with them. They did not recognize her, but looked at her with envy. The prince couldn't take his eyes off her and couldn't eat at all, such was the spell of her beauty.

When Cinderella heard the clock strike a quarter to twelve she made a curtsey to the whole assembly and then left as quickly as she could.

As she got home her fine ball dress transformed back into her ragged clothes, and everything else was changed back to its original state. She stored the pumpkin in the cellar together with the mice, the fat rat and the lizards and made sure they had plenty to eat and drink. "You deserve it," she said, and hurried back upstairs.

She thanked the old lady and wished that she might go to the ball the next evening, as the prince had invited her.

Just then the ugly sisters arrived home. The old lady instantly changed back into a cat and Cinderella quickly let her out of the back door.

"Oh, poor little Cinderella!" her sisters cried. "You should have been there. Such a grand ball. And the most gorgeous princess arrived unexpectedly and came and sat with us.

Cinderella asked the name of the princess but they told her nobody knew it and that the prince was greatly interested in her and would give the world to know who she could be.

"Was she very beautiful?" asked Cinderella, rather enjoying herself, "I wish I could see her for myself. Perhaps I could borrow one of your old dresses and go to the ball tomorrow evening?"

"What? Let a mucky little maid like you wear one of our dresses? You must think us mad."

But, next evening, Cinderella did go to the ball in her glittering coach accompanied by her loyal coachman and footmen. She was dressed even more magnificently than before. Again, her sisters failed to recognize her and, this time, the prince did not leave her side. He never stopped paying her the most loving attentions and they talked and laughed all evening. She so enjoyed his company that she forgot the old woman's instructions until she heard the chime of midnight.

She slipped from the prince's arms and flew away like a frightened fawn. She couldn't let him see her in her real clothes. The prince sprang after her but she was too swift for him. Only, as she fled down the stairs, she lost one of her glass slippers, which the prince tenderly picked up.

The prince asked the guards at the palace gate if they had seen a princess leave; they replied they had seen only a ragged young girl who looked more like a kitchen maid and seemed to be chasing some mice.

When the sisters arrived home from the ball, Cinderella asked them if the beautiful princess had been there again. They told her yes; but she had run away on the stroke of midnight, leaving behind one of her pretty glass slippers, which the prince had clutched to his heart for the rest of the evening.

A few days later, the prince sent trumpeters all over the the country to proclaim that he wished to marry whoever possessed the foot that fitted the slipper.

So the slipper was first tried on all the princesses, then on all the duchesses, and next on all the ladies of the court. It fitted none of them. Then it was tried on the feet of all the other ladies who had been at the ball.

At last, they brought the slipper to Cinderella's house. The two ugly sisters were waiting eagerly in the parlor. They each tried with all their might to squeeze a fat foot into the dainty slipper, but no matter how much they huffed and puffed, they could not manage it.

"I danced so much at the ball my little foot must have swollen," one of them said.

"Why, I danced even more than you," retorted the other sister as she screwed up her toes in a vain effort to fit the slipper.

Cinderella watched them. Then she laughed and said "I would like to try." Her sisters scoffed and teased her but the prince's envoy said, "Why not? I have been asked to try everyone in the kingdom."

Cinderella gently slipped her foot into the delicate shoe. The slipper fitted perfectly.

"That awful, grubby girl cannot possibly have been at the ball," snapped the stepmother. But then Cinderella drew the other glass slipper from her apron pocket and slipped it on.

Well! You can imagine the amazement on the faces of the sisters and their mother. And when a little old lady appeared and touched Cinderella's rags with her walking stick, transforming them into a dress even more magnificent than she had worn before, the sisters knelt before her and begged her to forgive them for all the bad treatment they had made her suffer.

Cinderella kissed them both and forgave them both with all her heart, and then, looking every inch the princess, she was taken through the cheering crowds to meet her prince.

The prince thought her more beautiful than ever and they married a few days later. Cinderella, who was as good as she was beautiful, brought her sisters to live with her in the palace and soon they also were married to great lords.

Cinderella never saw the old lady again, but the cat was always by her side. Every day Cinderella stroked the cat and said, "I know I owe all this happiness to you. I can never thank you enough."

But all the cat would say was, "Meow."

"With autumn came the rain, and
the three little pigs started to feel
they needed a proper home."

THE *Three Little* PIGS

Once upon a time there were three little pigs, who left their home to see the world. All summer long, they roamed through the woods and over the meadows, playing games and just having fun. They made friends with everyone they met and none were more happy than the three little pigs.

Then the summer days grew shorter and there was a chill in the evening air. Folk began drifting back to their jobs and preparing for winter. With autumn came the rain, and the three little pigs started to feel they needed a proper home. They realized, sadly, that the fun time was over and they must get to work like everyone else or they would find themselves out in the cold and wet, with no roof over their heads. But, what to do?

The laziest little pig said they should build a straw hut. "It'll only take a day," he said.

The others disagreed. "It will be too fragile," they said, but he refused to listen, and built one for himself anyway.

The second little pig went off and found an old wooden fence. "These planks will make a fine wooden house," he said and, Crash! Bang! Wallop! In two days he had finished his house.

But the third little pig did not approve of the wooden house. "That's no way to build a proper house," he said. "It takes time, and care, and hard work to build a house strong enough to withstand the wind and rain and snow. And most important of all, to protect us from the wicked wolf."

Slowly, day after day, the third little pig worked on his house and, day after day, and brick by brick, his house took shape. From time to time, his brothers came to see how he was getting on. They laughed

and said, "Why do you work so hard? Why don't you come and play?"

But the hardworking bricklaying pig said "Not until I have finished the house. I will not be foolish like you two, and he who laughs last, laughs longest."

One day, when the wise little pig went to the river to get water for his cement, he found the tracks of a big wolf. He sounded the alarm and the little pigs rushed to their homes and shut the doors tight.

Along came the big, bad wolf and glared angrily at the laziest pig's straw hut. "Come out!" he yelled. "Come out, or I'll huff and I'll puff, and I'll blow your house down!"

"If you don't mind, Mr. Wolf, I'd rather stay where I am," squealed the little pig.

"I do mind!" bellowed the wolf, and puffing out his hairy chest, he took a very deep breath. Then he blew with all his might and the sticks and straw of the hut swirled around the lazy little pig like a whirlwind and then fell in a heap on the ground.

"Now, where are you, my cheeky little pig? Roared the wolf. But the little pig had escaped in the confusion and was dashing as fast as his tiny trotters would allow, towards his brother's wooden house.

"Come back!" yelled the big, bad wolf but the two little pigs were already slamming shut the wooden door.

"I hope this house is strong enough! Let's lean against the door so he can't get in."

"Open up! Open up!" roared the wolf, punching and kicking the door. "I only want to chat with you." Inside the two brothers shook with fear and tried their hardest to keep the door shut tight.

"You're making me really angry, now!" warned the wolf. "If you won't open the door and have a friendly chat, I will huff and puff, and BLOW YOUR HOUSE DOWN!"

Again, he puffed out his hairy chest and sucked in a huge breath, and . . . WHOOOOSH! The wooden house collapsed around the two pigs like a pile of matchsticks.

However, the wise little pig had been watching the whole scene from his brick house and he quickly opened the door for his brothers fleeing from the wolf.

No sooner had he slammed the door shut behind them than the wolf began hammering on it.

"Open up, or I'll huff, and I'll puff, and I'LL BLOW YOUR HOUSE DOWN!"

Well, he huffed and he puffed, but he could not blow this house down. He tried, and he tried, until he felt quite dizzy. But he was a crafty old wolf, and he decided to try one of his tricks. He pulled up a length of fence and used it as a ladder to climb onto the roof, to see

if he could get down the chimney. But the wise little pig had seen the trick, and said, "Quick! Light the fire."

Now the wolf had both hind legs already into the chimney and was unsure what was beneath him, but he was hungry and the thought of not just one, not two, but three tasty little pigs was too tempting. He let himself drop. His landing was hot. Very hot! His tail caught fire and he ran away screaming, jumped into the river and was swept away

The three happy little pigs danced round and round and sang, "Ole! Ole! Mr. Wolf is washed away!"

Next day, the wise little pig helped his brothers start to build two new brick houses. The big, bad wolf did return once more to the neighborhood, but when he saw the three chimneys he was reminded of the pain in his burnt tail and went away forever. Now, safe and happy, the wise little pig turned to his brothers and said, "No more work! Come on, let's go and play."

"An old castle, ringed around by it's deep moat lay bathed in sunshine."

THE Ugly Duckling

 It was glorious out in the countryside. It was high summer and the corn was beginning to turn golden, the hay had been cut and put up in stacks in the meadows, and there the storks strutted about on their long red legs and chattered in Egyptian. All around the fields were great woods and hidden in the cool shade lay pools and deep lakes.

An old castle, ringed around by its deep moat, lay bathed in sunshine. Between the thick, crumbling walls and the edge of the moat there grew a forest of burdock plants, so high that a child could stand under them and imagine he was in the middle of the wild wood. Here a duck had built her nest.

She was feeling rather sorry for herself, sitting there, waiting for her eggs to hatch. It was taking an awfully long time and nobody came to visit her. The other ducks preferred swimming about and gossiping. Finally though, one eggshell began to crack. "Peep, peep," they cried as, one by one, little creatures stuck out their heads and blinked in the light.

"Quack, quack," said their mother. "Look around you." And the little ducklings looked around.

"How big the world is!" piped the young ones, and shook off the remains of their little shells.

"Do you think this is *all* the world?" quacked their mother. "No, it is much larger than this! It stretches right across the water and into that field. Now, are you all ready?" The duck got up and turned to look into her nest. There sat the biggest egg, still unhatched.

"Oh no," said mother duck gloomily. "I'm fed-up with sitting around. How long is this going to take?" And she sat back down.

The next day, an old duck decided to come visiting. "Well, how's it going?" she asked, admiring the little ducklings snuggling close to their mother.

"Oh, don't ask," groaned mother duck. "My biggest egg just won't crack. But just look at the others, aren't they the best-looking little ducklings you've ever seen? All the very image of their father, the rascal, who hasn't come to visit me once."

"Let's have a look at this egg, then," said the old visitor. Mother duck shuffled to the side and the visitor peered closely at the offending egg. "It's a turkey egg," she said confidently. "Just ignore it. Let it lie there. Go and teach your little ones how to swim."

"I think I'll sit on it just a little longer," said mother duck, not wanting to abandon the egg despite its reluctance to hatch. "I've sat here so long that I suppose I can manage another day or two."

Suddenly, the great egg burst with a loud crack. "Peep, peep," cried the young one and stumbled out. He was big and very ugly.

The mother duck was shocked. "He's awfully big," she thought.

"Perhaps he really is a turkey. There's one sure way to find out. Come along, children," and she waddled to the edge of the moat. SPLASH! She jumped into the water, and one duckling after another plunged in. The big ugly one stood on the edge for a moment, then he, too, went in with a great splash, and swam beautifully.

"No. That's no turkey," quacked mother duck. "Look how well he uses his legs, and how straight he holds his neck. He is my own child, and he is quite handsome, in an odd sort of way. Quack! Quack! Now follow me, and I'll take you to the farmyard and introduce you to everyone. Walk nicely and keep close together. And watch out for the cat."

When they arrived at the farmyard, there was a tremendous hullabaloo going on. Two families of ducks were squabbling over some scraps, and the cat ran off with them anyway.

"That naughty old cat," sighed the mother duck. "Now, be sure to bow to that old duck over there. She is the grandest of all here, and see the red ribbon tied around one of her legs? That shows that she is to be respected by everyone. Quack! Quack! Don't walk, waddle. Turn your toes out, stick your bottoms out and waddle like good ducks should. And so mother duck and her children waddled over and bowed politely to the duck with the red ribbon. The ducks who had been involved in the hullabaloo, now turned their attention to the newcomers.

"Who are this lot?" they said quite rudely. "There are enough of us here already trying to feed our families. We don't want more moving in."

"And look how ugly that one is!" quacked another. "We don't want him here. He'll eat up everything in a second and scare the little ones." He flew up and pecked the ugly duckling sharply.

"Leave him alone!" cried mother duck. "He's done no harm to anyone."

"He doesn't even look like a duckling!" replied the duck who had pecked him. "And that's reason enough to peck him."

"You have lovely ducklings," quacked the old duck with the red ribbon. And their behavior does you credit. But the big one didn't turn out very well."

"He lay too long in the egg, I think," answered the mother duck. "But he swims beautifully and has a friendly character. Besides, he is a drake and so good looks are not so important. He is strong and will make his way in the world."

"Well, the others are fine," said the old duck. "Make yourself at home; and if you find any scraps, you may bring them to me." And so mother duck and her family set up home in the farmyard, but the ugly duckling was teased by most of the ducks and all the chickens. The big turkey cock strutted over and flashed his spurs and shouted gobbledygook at him. The poor ugly duckling didn't know what to do. He was mocked and laughed at by the whole farmyard.

So it went the first day, and afterwards it became worse and worse for the ugly duckling. His own brothers and sisters were embarrassed by him and grew angry. "If only the cat would carry you off!" they said heartlessly.

Even his mother grew to regret staying on her nest. "If you were not here, we could get on with our lives in peace," she thought secretly.

The duckling became more and more miserable. At last he decided to run away. He rushed through the hedge, disturbing all the little birds who flew up into the air. "They are flying away because I am so ugly," he thought sadly.

Finally he came to a great marsh where the wild ducks lived and here he stayed for the night, tired, cold and very lonely. In the morning he was found by the wild ducks. "What sort of bird are you?" they asked rather rudely. The duckling bowed to them and tried to be as polite as possible. "I am a duck," he explained.

"You are too ugly to be a duck," laughed the wild ducks.

The duckling wished they would go away. All he wanted was to be allowed to live in peace, swim among the reeds and drink a little water when he was thirsty.

He stayed two days in the marsh; then two wild geese came. They were both young and rather brash and cheeky. "Listen," said one of the geese, "even though you're amazingly ugly, we like you. Come, fly with us. There's a marsh not far from here where some friends of ours live. We can go have some fun with them, and you never know, it could change your life, ugly though you are!"

Bang! Bang! Suddenly, two shots were heard and both geese fell

down dead, their blood turning the water red. Bang! Bang! Two more shots, and a flock of wild geese flew up. Bang! Bang! The whole marsh was surrounded by hunters and from every direction came the awful noise of gunfire. The blue smoke from the guns drifted like a fog over the water, and hunting dogs came splashing through the marsh.

The little duckling was terrified. He was about to tuck his head under his wing and try to hide, when he saw a huge dog peering down at him with eyes mad with excitement. The dog bared its great teeth, and then, splash, splash, on it went without touching the duckling. "Oh, thank heavens," thought the duckling. "I am so ugly that even the dog doesn't want me."

The little duckling lay quietly while the shots whistled through the reeds. At last, late in the day, the shooting stopped and the hunters and dogs splashed away, and silence returned to the marsh. Still the little duckling was too frightened to move, and waited several hours before taking his head out from under his wing. Then he hastened away out of the marsh and across a wide, desolate moor.

Thunder rumbled behind dark clouds. A strong wind got up and whipped rain into the face of the little duckling which he could hardly move against. Towards evening he came to a poor little hut. The hut was so crooked that it did not know which way to fall down, and so remained standing… just. The door was hanging off one hinge and he squeezed inside and lay quietly in the dark. An old woman lived in the hut with her cat and her hen. The cat was called Sonny and sparks flew off his shiny coat if it was rubbed the wrong way. The hen had very short legs and that was why she was called Cluck Lowlegs. She was good at laying eggs, and the old woman loved her like a child.

In the morning the duckling was discovered by the cat who meowed, and the hen started clucking. "What is all the fuss about?" asked the old woman. She couldn't see very well, and when she saw the overgrown duckling, she thought it was a fat, full-grown duck. "What a fine catch!" she cried. "Now we shall have duck eggs, unless it's a drake. We'll give it a try." So the duckling was allowed to stay for three weeks to see if it could lay eggs.

The cat thought himself master of the house, and the hen was the mistress. They thought of themselves as the finest things in the world. When the duckling tried to express a different opinion, the cat simply said, "Do your feathers make sparks?"

And the hen said, "Can you lay eggs?"

"No."

"Well, in that case, don't interrupt when sensible folk are talking." So the duckling sat glumly in the corner until a little beam of sunshine shone through the gap in the door. Suddenly he remembered how lovely it was to be out and swimming in the brightness of day. He was so overcome by the urge to plunge into cool sparkling water that he couldn't help talking about it.

"What are you chattering about?" the hen asked. "You have nothing to do, except get daft ideas like that. Lay eggs or make sparks, and you will have no time for such silly notions."

"You have no idea how wonderful it is to float in the water, or dive right down to the bottom of a lake," cried the duckling.

"You must have gone mad," said the hen. "Ask the cat—he is the most intelligent creature I know—ask him whether he likes to swim or dive down to the bottom of a lake. And ask the old woman—who is the cleverest person in the world—ask her whether she likes to float about and get her head all wet."

"You don't understand me," said the duckling.

"We don't understand *you*! I hope you don't think you are wiser than the cat or the old woman—not to mention myself. Now get to work; lay some eggs, or learn to make some sparks."

"I think I'll go out into the wide world," replied the duckling.

"Push off, then," said the hen. "Go right ahead!"

So the duckling left the hut and found a lake where he could swim and dive again. There were other ducks there, but the little duckling wasn't surprised when they ignored him, and he was happy to be left in peace.

Autumn came and the leaves turned gold and brown, and then fell from the trees and danced in the breeze. The clouds hung low and heavy with snow. The only sound in the silent landscape was a raven that sat on a fence and screeched, "Gwark! Gwark!" in the cold. Just think how miserable the lonely duckling must have been.

One evening, as the sun was setting in all its glory, a flock of beautiful birds emerged from among the reeds. Their feathers were dazzlingly white, and they had long graceful necks. They were swans.

They uttered a loud cry and spread their glorious great wings and flew away from the cold to the warm countries of the south, where the lakes remain free from ice in the winter. Higher and higher they circled. The ugly duckling turned round and round in the water and stretched his neck up towards the sky, and tried to flap his little wings. He felt a strange longing.

Oh, he would never forget those beautiful happy birds. He did not know what they were called, nor where they were going, and yet he felt he loved them more than any other creatures he had ever met.

The winter grew colder and colder. The duckling had to swim round and round in the water to prevent the surface from freezing over. Each night, his hole in the ice became smaller and smaller. The little duckling had to keep his feet moving the whole time, but at last he became exhausted, and lay still. The ice closed in around him and he was frozen fast.

There he would have died, but luck was on his side for once. Early the next morning, a passing farmer saw the frozen duckling and broke the ice with his wooden shoe to free the poor creature. The man tucked the bird under his arm and carried him home to his wife, who warmed him near the fire. The children wanted to play with him, but the duckling was afraid and flapped his wings and flew, splash, into the milk pail. From there he flew, splosh, into a big bowl of butter and then, spluff, into a barrel of flour. What a sight he was!

The farmer's wife chased him with a broom. The children laughed and fell over each other, trying to catch him. Fortunately, the door was open, and he escaped into the yard and hid behind the woodpile. From there he slipped quietly away in the softly falling snow, towards the open moor.

It would be too sad to tell of all the hardship and suffering the little duckling endured during that long winter. But he made a nest as best he could from reeds and moss, and he survived. When the sun began

to shine again, and the larks to sing, Spring brought warmth and hope to the duckling. He flapped his wings, and they beat the air more strongly than before, and he felt a great lifting and soaring, and he was up, high above the moor, riding on his very own breeze!

Before he knew how it happened, he was far from the moor and flying over a beautiful garden. Apple trees were in blossom and willow trees stretched their fresh green branches over the water of a winding canal. Out from a thicket of rushes came three swans. They floated lightly on the water and the duckling flew down toward them. "I know these royal creatures will not want me near them. They will probably attack me, but no matter. It can't get much worse for me." He landed on the water and swam toward the magnificent swans. When they saw him they ruffled their feathers and stretched wide their enormous wings and started to swim toward him. He bowed his head low toward the water and waited for the sharp words and pecks that he was sure would come. But what was that he saw in the water? It was his own reflection; and he was no longer a big, awkward, ugly bird. He looked just like these gracious, majestic birds. He was a swan!

The swans formed a circle around him and caressed him with their beaks. Since he had suffered so much, it made him appreciate his new happiness all the more. Children came into the garden to feed the swans. The youngest child shouted, "Look, there's a new one." The children clapped and cheered, and ran to tell their parents. Cake and bread were thrown onto the water for them, and everyone agreed that the new swan was the most beautiful of all.

He was so happy, but he was also shy. He hid his head beneath his wing.

He thought of the times he had been teased for looking strange, and now everyone said he was the most beautiful of the most beautiful of birds. The sun sparkled on the water around him and the willows bowed their heads towards him. He ruffled his feathers and raised his long slender neck to the blue of the sky. He was so happy, but not proud. He had the same kind heart he had when he was the ugly duckling; and a kind heart can never be too proud.

"Long ago in deep mid winter, a queen
sat sewing beside a window."

Snow WHITE

Long ago, in deep mid winter, a queen sat sewing beside a window; a window with a black ebony frame. And as she was sewing and looking out at the falling snow, she pricked her finger and three drops of blood fell on the snow.

The red looked so beautiful on the white snow and she thought to herself how lovely it would be to have a child as white as snow, with cheeks so red and hair as black as ebony.

Before winter came again, the queen gave birth to a baby girl who was as white as snow, with blood red cheeks and with hair as black as ebony. They called her Snow White, and as the baby was born, the queen died.

A year or more later, the king married again. His new queen was beautiful, but very proud, and couldn't bear the thought that any one might be more beautiful than she. She had a magic mirror and when she stood in front of it and said:

"Mirror, mirror on the wall,

Who is the fairest one of all?"

The mirror would reply:

"My Lady Queen, you are the fairest one of all."

Then the queen was very happy because she knew the mirror always told the truth.

However, Snow White was growing up more beautiful every day. By the time she was seven years old she was as beautiful as a spring day and so, when the queen next asked the mirror:

"Mirror, mirror on the wall,

Who is the fairest one of all?"

The mirror answered:

"My Lady Queen, you're the fairest here,

But Snow White is a thousand times more fair."

The queen gasped and grew mad with envy. From that moment on, every time she saw Snow White the pride and envy within her body grew like weeds around her heart so that she couldn't rest by day or by night.

Finally, she sent for a huntsman and said, "Get that child out of my sight. Take her to the forest and kill her and bring me her lungs and liver to prove you've done it."

The servant took Snow White off to the forest, but when he drew his hunting knife and prepared to pierce the child's innocent heart, she began to cry and said, "Dear huntsmen, let me live. I'll run off into the wild woods and never come home again."

Because she was so young, the huntsman had pity and said, "Run away then, little one." Though he thought to himself, "The wild beasts of the forest will soon eat you up." Not having to kill her eased his conscience a little.

Just then the huntsman spotted a young boar amongst the trees. He chased and caught it and cut out its lungs and liver and took them back to the queen as proof that he had done as she wished. Then the palace cook was ordered to stew them up with plenty of salt and pepper and the evil queen ate them up.

Meanwhile, Snow White was all alone in the forest and didn't know what to do. So she began to run, and run, and run. She ran through thorny thickets and over sharp stones. She saw wild beasts rushing about, but they did not harm her. She ran as far as her legs would carry her, and then, just as the daylight was fading, she came to a little house. The door opened to her touch and she went in to rest.

Everything in the little house was tiny, but wonderfuly neat and clean. A little table was laid with a white cloth and seven little plates, each with its own knife, fork and spoon, and seven little mugs. Over against the wall were seven little beds all in a row, each covered with a snowy white sheet.

Snow White was hungry and thirsty and she looked at the food on the seven little plates and wondered what was in the seven little mugs. She didn't want to eat up someone's entire meal so she ate a tiny piece of bread and a tiny piece of cheese and a little salad from each of the plates and hoped no one would notice. Then she had a sip of wine from each of the mugs and felt sleepy. (She had never had wine before.) She lay down on one of the beds, but none of the beds suited her. They were too long, or too short, or too hard, or too soft. Except the seventh one. It was perfect, and soon Snow White was fast asleep.

When it was really, really dark in the deep dark wood, the owners of the little house came home. They were seven dwarfs who went off to the mountains every day to dig and tunnel for silver and gold. When they lit their seven little candles they knew that someone had been there because the house was not as neat and tidy as they had left it.

The first dwarf said "Who's been sitting in my chair?"

And the second, "Who's been eating from my little plate?"

The third, "Whose been nibbling my bread?"

The fourth, "Who's been eating my salad?"

The fifth, "Whose been using my little fork?"

And the sixth said, "Who's been cutting with my little knife?"

The seventh dwarf said, "Who's been drinking from my little mug?"

Then the first dwarf looked around and saw a hollow in his bed. "Whose been laying on my little bed?" he cried.

Then they all looked and gasped, "Someone's been on my bed, too!"

But the seventh looked at his bed and said, "Sssh! Someone is sleeping in my bed!" And they all held up their seven candles and let the light fall on Snow White.

"Heavens above," they said, "what a beautiful child!" They were so delighted they didn't wake her but let her go on sleeping in the little bed. The seventh dwarf slept with the others – one hour with each – until the night was over.

Next morning Snow White woke up and when she saw the seven dwarfs she was frightened, but they smiled at her and asked her name.

"I am called Snow White," she said. When they asked her how she came to be in their little house she told them of the evil queen who wanted to kill her and how she had run and run until, at last,

she had come upon their home. The dwarfs were in tears when they heard her sad story and they said, "If you will keep house for us and cook and keep everything neat and clean, you can stay with us and want for nothing."

"Oh yes," said Snow White and gratefully accepted their hospitality. So she kept house for them, and every morning the seven dwarfs went off to the mountains, looking for silver and gold, warning Snow White not to open the door to anyone. Every evening they returned and Snow White would have their supper ready.

Now—remember that evil queen?—well, after eating what she thought was Snow White's lungs and liver, she felt sure that she was again the most beautiful of all. She stood in front of her mirror and said:

"Mirror, mirror, here I stand,

Who is the fairest in the land?"

And the mirror is replied:

"You, O Queen, are the fairest here,

But Snow White, who has gone to stay

With the seven dwarfs far, far away

Is a thousand times more fair."

"What!" the queen gasped. She knew the mirror told no lies and that the huntsman had deceived her. Snow White was still alive!

The queen stormed about the palace and could not rest until she had thought of a way of destroying Snow White. At last she thought of a plan and disguised herself as an old peddler woman and filled a basket with pretty ribbons and silks and laces and made her way over the seven hills to the house of the seven dwarfs.

She knocked on the door and cried out, "Pretty things for sale! Fine things for sale!"

Snow White peeped out of the window and called, "Good lady, old lady, what do you have to sell?"

"Nice things, lovely things," she replied, "laces, all colors," and she waved a lace of many colored silk.

"Well," thought Snow White, "surely I can let in an honest looking old lady like her," and she unbolted the door and bought the lace.

"Dear child," said the old woman, "let me lace you up properly."

"You're very kind," said Snow White and turned her back so that the old woman could lace her bodice with the new ribbon. But the old woman laced quick and she laced tight, so tight that Snow White lost all the breath in her body and fell to the ground as if dead.

"Well, my beauty!" said the queen, "and who is the fairest in the land, now?" And she hurried away.

Meanwhile, the dwarfs came out of the mine to find the sky had turned dark and stormy. Thunder echoed through the valleys and the forest. Worried about Snow White they hurried down the mountain to their home.

They were horrified when they found their beloved Snow White lying on the floor, so still they thought she was dead. They lifted her up and when they saw she was too tightly laced, they cut the lace. She breathed just a little and slowly came back to life again.

"You can be sure that the old woman was none other than the wicked queen," they said.

When the wicked queen got home she went to the mirror and asked:

"Mirror, mirror, on the wall
Who is the fairest one of all?"

And the mirror answered as usual:

"You, O Queen, are the fairest here,
But Snow White, who has gone to stay
With the Seven dwarfs far, far away,
Is a thousand times more fair."

When she heard that, all the blood drained from her face and she turned a livid green, for she knew Snow White had recovered.

"Just wait, child," she hissed to herself, "this time I will think of something to destroy you for ever."

With the help of some magic spells, she made a poisonous comb. Then she disguised herself as yet another old woman and made her way over the seven hills to the home of the seven dwarfs. She knocked on the door and called out:

"Pretty things for sale!"

"Go away, I'm not allowed to let you in."

"You can look, my child, can't you?" said the old woman, taking out the poisoned comb and holding it up so that it glinted in the sunlight. Snow White liked it so much that she forgot what the dwarfs had told her, and she unbolted the door.

When they had agreed the price, the old woman offered to comb Snow White's hair and the child agreed. Most little girls like having their hair brushed and combed. As soon as the comb touched her hair the poison started to work and Snow White fell to the floor.

"Hair today, gone tomorrow," cackled the old woman and hurried away.

Luckily it wasn't long 'til nightfall and the seven dwarfs were soon home and found Snow White lying on the floor as if dead. They found the poisoned comb tangled in her hair, and no sooner had they carefully pulled it out, than she woke up.

"Dear child," they said, "You must never open the door to anyone."

When the queen got home she went to the mirror and said:

"Mirror, mirror, here I stand,

Who is the fairest in the land?"

And the mirror answered as before:

"You, O Queen, are the fairest here,

But with Snow White, who has gone to stay

With the seven dwarfs far, far away,

Is a thousand times more fair."

When she heard the mirror say that, she shook with rage.

"Snow White, you shall die! Even if it costs me my own life." Then she went to a secret room high in a tower of her castle and made a deadly poisonous apple. She put it into a basket with other apples and, when she had disguised herself as an old peasant woman, hurried over the seven hills to the house of the seven dwarfs.

When Snow White heard the knock at the door, she leaned out of the window and called out, "I'm not opening the door. The seven dwarfs have told me not to."

"That's all right, dear. I don't want to come in. I just want to get rid of these beautiful apples. I have more than I need. Here, I'll give you one."

"No. No thank you," said Snow White. "I'm not allowed to take anything."

"What!" said the peasant woman, "you don't think they're poisoned do you? Look, I'll cut this one in half and we can share it."

She cut the apple in half and offered the shiny red half to Snow White, for the apple was so cleverly made that only the red portion was poisoned.

"Here," the peasant woman said, "as rosy red as your cheeks."

When Snow White saw the peasant eating the green half of the apple, she stretched out her hand for the red half. As soon as she had a single bite she fell to the floor.

When the queen looked in the window and saw Snow White lying still and lifeless, she laughed a mad, terrible laugh and said, "White as snow, red as blood, black as ebony. The dwarfs won't revive you this time."

She hurried home and stood in front of her mirror:

>"Mirror, mirror, here I stand,
>
>Who is the fairest in the land?"

The mirror answered, at last:

>"You, O Queen, are the fairest in the land."

And so, at last, her evil envious heart was satisfied, at least as far as an envious heart can ever be satisfied.

When the seven dwarfs came home that evening they found Snow White lying there. They lifted her up, looked for anything poisonous, unlaced her, combed her hair and, at dawn, washed her face with early morning dew, but nothing helped. The dear child was dead, and dead she remained. All seven sat around and wept for three days.

Then they were going to bury her, but she still looked so alive and still had her beautiful red cheeks.

"We cannot bury such a beauty in the black earth," they said and they had a coffin made of glass so that she could be seen from all sides. They wrote her name in gold letters on the coffin saying that she was the daughter of a king.

Then they placed the coffin on a mountain top, and one of them always stayed there to guard it. Beasts from the forest and birds came and wept for Snow White, owls, ravens and doves.

For a long, long time she lay in her coffin, unchanging in the passing years; as white as snow, as red as blood, with hair as black as ebony. Then, one day, a prince travelling through the forest came to the house of the seven dwarfs and asked if he could stay for the night.

In the morning he saw the glass coffin on the mountain with the beautiful Snow White inside.

He begged the dwarfs to sell him the coffin. "I will give you whatever you ask for," he said. But the dwarfs said they wouldn't part with it for all the money in the world. "Then give it to me and I will love and cherish her forever. I don't think I can go on living if I cannot look upon such beauty."

When the dwarfs heard these words they looked kindly upon the prince and said he could take the coffin to his palace, where

he promised it would lay in a room of cool marble overlooking a beautiful garden.

The prince called his servants to hoist the glass coffin onto their shoulders but, as they were carrying it away, they stumbled on the rough ground. The jolt shook the poisoned piece of apple out of Snow White's throat. Within a moment, she lifted the crystal lid of the coffin and sat up. To the joy and astonishment of everyone there, she was alive again.

"Where am I?" she cried.

"With me!" the young prince answered joyfully, "With me!" Then he told her what had happened and said, "I have never seen such beauty. I love you more than anything in the world. Come home to my father's castle and be my wife."

Their wedding was to be magnificent and the seven dwarfs were guests of honor. Among the other guests was Snow White's wicked stepmother and when she was dressed and ready in her wedding finery, she stepped in front of her mirror and said,

"Mirror, mirror, here I stand,

Who is the fairest in the land?"

And the mirror answered:

"You O Queen, are the fairest here,

But the new young queen is a thousand times more fair."

When she heard that, she kicked the mirror, spat out a curse and raged up and down the room. She didn't know what to do with herself. At first she didn't want to go to the wedding at all, but then she just couldn't resist seeing the young queen.

The moment she entered the wedding hall she recognised Snow White, and she was speechless with horror. Then she screamed and tore her hair and ripped her fine dress, then ran yelling and cursing out of the castle and into the forest where the birds and the beasts remembered how she had treated Little Snow White.

By the time they had finished with the evil queen nothing much remained: just a few drops of blood, bones as white as snow, and her heart as black as ebony.

"...the youngest son was left with the cat,
and he was most disappointed."

Puss in BOOTS

Once upon a time a poor miller died and had only three things to leave to his three sons; the old mill, a donkey and a cat. The oldest son got the mill, the middle son got the donkey, and the youngest son was left with the cat, and he was most disappointed.

"My brothers can both earn a living with their inheritance, but what use is a cat?" he asked in some despair.

"Don't be sad, master," said the cat to the young lad. I'm worth more than an old mill or a mangy donkey. Just give me a pair of boots to protect my feet, a bag and a hat with a feather and see what I can do."

The boy was not too surprised as it was quite common for cats to speak in those days, and gave the cat what he wanted.

"Well, my fine Puss in Boots," he said, "show me what you can do."

With a wave of his new hat, Puss strode away in his new boots and soon caught a fat rabbit and popped it into his bag.

Then he walked up the hill to the castle, and banged on the door and asked to see the king. The guards and courtiers were impressed by the cat in his boots and feathered hat, and showed him into the presence of the king.

"Sire," he said, removing his hat with a sweeping bow, "the famous Marquis of Carabas sends you this fine plump rabbit as a gift."

"Oh," said the king. "Please thank your master."

"'Til tomorrow," replied Puss with another elaborate bow.

Next day Puss hid in a cornfield and bagged two fat partridges which he took to the king. "Sire, another gift from the Marquis of Carabas."

The king accepted the partridges and gave Puss a good tip for his trouble.

In the days that followed, Puss regularly visited the castle with his bag full of rabbits, partridges, hares and skylarks, presenting them all to the king in the name of the famous Marquis of Carabas. The folk at the castle began to talk about this mysterious Marquis.

"He must be a great hunter," said one.

"And he is very loyal to the king," remarked another, "and so generous."

"But who is he?" asked another. I've never heard heard of him."

The queen was most interested in this generous nobleman. "Is your master young and handsome?" she asked Puss.

"Oh yes. And very rich too," answered Puss. "In fact, he would be honored if you and the king called to see him in his palace."

When Puss returned home and told his master that the king and queen were going to visit he was horrified. "Why did you invite them?" he cried. "As soon as they see me they will know how poor I am."

"Don't worry," said Puss in Boots, "I have a plan."

For several days Puss continued taking gifts to the king and queen and one day heard that the royal couple were taking the princess on a carriage ride beside the river that very afternoon.

Puss hurried home in great excitement. "Master, master, it is time to carry out my plan. You must go for a swim in the river immediately."

"But I can't swim," cried the young man worriedly.

Don't worry," replied Puss. "Just trust me."

So they went to the river and when the royal carriage appeared Puss pushed his master into the water.

"Help! Help!" cried Puss, "the Marquis of Carabas is drowning!"

The king put his head out of the carriage window and recognized the cat who had brought all the gifts.

"Save the Marquis!" shouted the king and sent his escorts to the rescue. While they were pulling the young lad out of the river, the cat went to the king's carriage and told how robbers had stolen his master's clothes while he swam. In fact the crafty cat had hidden the clothes under a rock.

The king ordered that a selection of his finest clothes be brought from the castle for the Marquis of Carabas to wear. When the young man put them on he looked extremely handsome and the princess certainly noticed.

"Wouldn't you like to marry such a man?" asked the queen.

"Oh yes!" replied the princess.

However, Puss heard one of the king's ministers remark that they must find out how rich he was. "Very, very rich," said Puss. "He owns the castle over the hill and all this land. Come and see for yourselves. I will meet you at the castle."

With these words, Puss rushed off in the direction of the castle. As he ran, he passed by some peasants in a hayfield, harvesters in a cornfield and a another group working in an orchard. To all of them he shouted, "If anyone asks you who your master is, answer 'the Marquis of Carabas.' He owns all this land now and he's very fierce. If you want to keep your jobs you must pledge allegiance to him."

Meanwhile, the king invited the Marquis to join them in the royal carriage and they drove on in style. When they came to a group of peasants piling up the bales of hay in a hayfield the king asked them who owned the field. "The Marquis of Carabas!" they all chorused.

And when they came to the harvesters in a cornfield bundling up the corn, the chorus was the same. "The Marquis of Carabas!" And when they enquired of workers in the orchard picking the apples, the answer was the same. "The Marquis of Carabas!"

"You have a fine estate," remarked the king.

"Yes, your majesty," replied the young man. "It surprises me how fine it has become."

Ahead of the royal party, at last the cat arrived at the castle. Now, in this castle lived an ogre, huge, cruel and extraordinarily rich; he was the true owner of all the land through which the king had travelled.

When the great door opened, Puss bowed low and exclaimed, "My Lord Ogre, my respects!"

"What do you want, cat?" growled the ogre.

"My Lord, I've heard that you possess wonderful powers. That, for instance, you can transform yourself into a lion or an elephant."

"I can," said the ogre, turning into a terrifying lion. He roared loudly and shook his mane and gnashed his terrible teeth. "So what?"

"Well," said Puss, shaking in his boots, "I have also heard that you can change into a tiny creature, like a mouse. And, forgive me, my Lord, but I think that must be impossible."

"Oh, you do, do you? Watch this then!" said the huge ogre, eager to show off, and changed into a tiny mouse.

Quick as a flash, the cat pounced on the mouse and gobbled him up.

Then Puss heard the sound of carriage wheels approaching and ran to greet the king and the royal party.

"Welcome, your Majesty, to the castle of the Marquis of Carabas."

The king was most impressed and he turned to the miller's son and said, "My dear Marquis, you're a fine, handsome young man, you have a magnificent castle and a great deal of land. Tell me, are you married?"

"No, sire," the young man answered and, looking at the princess, said, "but I would like to find a wife." The princess smiled at him and the queen clapped her hands together.

"Oh! I love a good wedding!" she cried.

And so the miller's son, now the Marquis of Carabas, married the princess and they lived happily in the great castle.

And Puss, who could now have as many feathered hats and pairs of boots as he could ever wish for, never wore hats nor boots again. He was happy just being a cat, curling up on the princess's lap, and occasionally reminding his master that a cat is worth much more than a mangy donkey or an old mill, any day.

"Rushing outside into the garden, she found
him laying by her favorite rose bush."

Beauty AND THE Beast

 Once upon a time there was a rich merchant who had three sons and three daughters and he gave them the best that money could buy. All the girls were pretty, and the youngest was the prettiest of all. When she was a baby, her family gave her the nickname "Little Beauty." As she grew older this was shortened to Beauty.

Beauty was not only the prettiest of the three sisters, she was also kind and thoughtful. The older sisters liked to mingle with the rich and famous; dancing at the grandest balls, sitting in the most expensive seats at the theatre, and strolling with the high and mighty in the park. Beauty preferred to stay at home with a good book.

Rich business men were always proposing marriage to the sisters but the two older ones said they would only marry a prince or a duke. Beauty always thanked everyone politely for their proposals but said she was too young and wished to stay with her father a little while longer.

Then, on one dreadful day, the merchant's business collapsed and he lost everything. No money was left. All he had now was a small house far away in the countryside. He tearfully told his family that there was nothing else to do but go and dig the land and grow their own food. The two elder sisters announced they would not leave the big city but would accept one of their marriage proposals. But now the sisters were no longer rich, none of their former suitors would even look at them.

All the folk in the city who had been upset by the older sisters' snooty ways said, "Let them go and be high and mighty among the sheep and pigs."

But there was sympathy for kind, gentle Beauty. All the rich men who had asked her to marry them proposed again, but she told them she could not possibly leave her father in his misfortune. She must work beside him in the countryside and comfort him in his sadness.

When they arrived at their new home, the merchant and his sons set to work on the land, and Beauty cooked and baked and cleaned and did all she could to help. At first she was exhausted by all this work, but gradually she grew stronger and the fresh country air made her feel healthier than ever before. She still missed the nice things that money had bought her but she told herself, "Crying won't do any good. I shall try to be happy without a penny."

Her two sisters were quite the opposite. They crawled out of bed at noon and spent their days moaning about the loss of their fancy city life and grand friends. They didn't lift a finger to help Beauty, but teased her, instead, for becoming such a housemaid.

The family lived in this way for almost a year, and then the merchant received news that a ship carrying valuable goods of his, that he had believed lost in a storm, had finally arrived safe in port. The good news immediately prompted the eldest girls to demand presents and asked their father to bring back new dresses and hats and all sorts of jewelery.

"You haven't asked me to bring you anything, Beauty," said her father.

Now Beauty thought her father couldn't possibly sell his cargo for enough money to buy even half the presents her sisters wanted, so she said, "Just bring yourself back home, safe and sound, and if you should see a rose, bring me a rose to remind me of the summer."

So the merchant set off, but when he came to the port he found that his precious cargo had already been distributed amongst his creditors to pay off his debts. After a great deal of argument, he had to start the long journey home just as poor as when he set out. When he was about an hour away from home he was caught in a fierce snowstorm.

Twice he was blown from his horse and as night closed in and wolves began howling all around, both horse and rider became hopelessly lost in a great wood.

The merchant began to lose hope of ever seeing his family again, and then he saw a light! As he went towards it he saw it shone from the windows of a magnificent palace. To his surprise he found the palace gates open and the courtyard empty. His weary horse saw the stable door stood ajar and, going inside, began to munch the oats and hay which looked as though they had been specially provided for him. After seeing his horse was fed and comfortable with a lush bed of straw, the merchant entered the palace. The massive door swung open

at a touch to reveal the great hall, a roaring fire and a long table bearing a feast of delicious things to eat. There was one place setting and one chair, but still no one to be seen.

The merchant stood dripping wet and steaming before the fire. "Surely the master of such a splendid place will forgive me for seeking warmth and shelter from the storm." He waited and waited, warming his front and his rear, but still no one, not even a servant appeared. The clock struck eleven and the merchant edged closer to the table, the smell of food making his empty stomach groan. He picked up a roast leg of chicken and looked around hoping to see someone so that he might say please, but still there was no one.

The chicken leg tasted so good that he couldn't resist eating the whole bird and washed it down with a glass of wine. Still no sign of anyone! "Even if the master is away there must be servants somewhere," he thought, and wandered from the great hall into the adjoining rooms. "Hello!" he called. "Anyone home?"

All of the magnificent rooms were deserted. At the top of a wide staircase he came to a room with a bed, the covers turned back and with large inviting pillows. He heard the clock strike midnight and, exhausted, he lay down to sleep.

When he woke next morning he was amazed to find a new set of clothes laid out for him. "Oh, thank you, thank you, whoever you are!" cried the merchant. From the window he saw no sign of snow, only parkland full of flowers. When he had dressed in his smart new outfit he went down to the great hall expecting to meet his generous host at last. Still there was no one to be seen, but on a table near the fire was a pot of hot chocolate and fresh pastries.

"Surely this palace must belong to a kind fairy who has taken pity on me," he thought. "Thank you kind fairy!" he said out loud. "Thank you for everything!" He finished off his breakfast and went to the stable for his horse. He passed by a rose tree and remembered his promise to Beauty. He reached up and picked a small bunch of flowers. Immediately there was a terrible roaring and suddenly before him appeared a beast so terrifying that the merchant fell to his knees in fright.

"Is this how you repay my kindness?" boomed the Beast. "I saved your life, gave you the freedom of my home and now you repay me by stealing what I love most in the world, my roses! Ungrateful wretch, you shall die!"

The merchant threw himself flat on the ground before the Beast. "Forgive me, my Lord. Forgive me. I picked them for one of my daughters who desired a rose above any other gift.

"Don't call me 'Lord,'" growled the Beast. "I am a Beast and flattery will get you nowhere. You say you have a daughter who loves roses. I would like to spare your life—but only on one condition, that this daughter comes here to die in your place!"

"No! Not my daughter!" exclaimed the merchant.

"Don't argue with me," said the Beast, "go before I change my mind. If your daughter refuses to die for you, swear you will return here in three months time."

The merchant had no intention of allowing his beautiful daughter to fall into the clutches of such a frightening creature but he promised to return. At least he would have some time to hold his family in his arms once more. Then the Beast's angry expression

softened. "I won't allow a guest of mine to leave empty handed," he said. "Next to the bed where you slept you will find an empty chest. Fill it with whatever pleases you, and it will be delivered to your home."

Then the Beast departed, and the merchant returned to the bedroom, telling himself that although he was to die, at least his beloved children would not starve. He found the empty chest and beside it was a great heap of golden coins. The golden coins filled the chest to the brim, exactly.

He let his horse find its own way home. Through his tears, he saw his sons and daughters running to greet him. The Beast had allowed him to keep Beauty's roses, and when he gave them to her and spoke of the terrible price he would have to pay, the elder sisters cried floods of tears and said it was all Beauty's fault.

"Why couldn't she have asked for pretty dresses like we did? Oh no! She had to be different. And now she's got Daddy into this awful trouble, and she's not even sorry!"

"Crying won't help," said Beauty. "And if the Beast will take me instead of a father, I shall willingly go."

"Never!" cried her three brothers. "We will find this creature and kill him."

"I doubt that is possible," said their father. "The Beast is not only big and terrifying but I'm sure he has special powers. Beauty, I will never allow you to sacrifice yourself for me. I am old and have lived my life. My only regret will be leaving you, my dears."

"I won't let you go by yourself," said Beauty. "And you can't stop me following you."

Beauty was determined and nothing would dissuade her. "I am young but I wouldn't want to live the rest of my life knowing I had caused the death of my father."

When the dreaded day came, the two elder sisters rubbed their eyes with onions to make a few tears when they said good bye to Beauty. The three brothers wept with open hearts. Beauty remained calm so that she wouldn't make them feel worse. They arrived at the palace as night fell, and the merchant saw the same guiding light through the trees. Once again the horse settled down in the stable, and the merchant led his daughter to the great hall. They found the same table spread with fine food but, this time, two places were set, not one.

Neither father nor daughter had any appetite but Beauty thought it might anger the Beast if they declined the food entirely, and served first her father and then herself. She thought, "Perhaps the Beast provided such a spread because he wants to fatten me up before he eats me." Then they heard a heavy tread and the creaking of stairs. Beauty shuddered when she saw the Beast. When he asked her if she had come of her own free will she answered, "Yes" in what she hoped was a brave, steady voice, although her blood froze and her whole body trembled.

The Beast bowed his head slightly. "I am very touched," he said, and turning to the merchant added, "And you, dear sir, must leave tomorrow and never come back. Goodnight Beauty." With another bow to both of them he was gone.

The merchant hugged his daughter. "Leave me here," he pleaded. "I am half dead with terror already. Leave me and save yourself."

"No father," insisted Beauty. "You will go home tomorrow morning and Heaven will protect me."

Then they went to bed, and although both feared they would not sleep a wink, as soon as their heads touched the pillows their eyes closed. Beauty dreamed of a beautiful lady who said, "Your bravery has pleased me Beauty. You will be rewarded." In the morning she told her father of her dream and it cheered him slightly as his horse carried him sadly home.

Beauty feared for the whole day that the Beast would eat her up that evening. Determined not to spend her last hours on earth moping and feeling sorry for herself, she began to explore the palace. Every room was grand and beautiful, and then she came to a door marked: 'Beauty's Room'. When she entered, the splendor took her breath away. Around three of the walls were big bookcases, and in front of high windows overlooking the park, stood a golden harp and many volumes of music. "Why would the Beast prepare such a wonderful room with so many books and so much music for someone he plans to eat this evening?" she wondered to herself. She took a book from a bookcase and gasped at the title. On the cover, written in gold letters, were the words "Beauty: Ask for whatever you wish. Here you are mistress of everything."

"All I want is to see my father and family again," she thought sadly. Suddenly, reflected in the glass door of the bookcase, appeared her father returning home and being greeted by her snivelling sisters and hugged by her weeping brothers. Then the image disappeared. "How thoughtful of the Beast to show me my father's safe return," thought Beauty. "Perhaps he is not all bad." At noon she found a delicious lunch on the long table and sweet music played all through the palace but without any sign of musicians.

When Beauty next sat at the table it was evening and she could hear the Beast roaring in a distant part of the palace. She trembled when the clock struck nine. She heard the creaking of the stair and his shadow fell across the food.

"May I watch you eat your supper, Beauty?" he asked quietly.

"Of course," replied Beauty politely but with a shaking voice.

"I don't wish to frighten you," said the Beast. "If my company offends you, you have only to tell me and I will leave." The Beast paused, and looked away for a moment. "You must think I am very ugly."

"Well, yes, I do" said Beauty, for she could not lie. Then she saw the pained look on his face and added, "But I think you are kind, too."

"I am ugly, and I am a fool," said the Beast. "A fool to think anyone could see beyond this terrifying face."

"A real fool would never admit that," replied Beauty. "I think your wild body hides a good heart. When I think of how thoughtful you have been, you do not frighten me."

"A good heart I may have," said the Beast, "but I am still a monster."

"I like you more with that ugly face of yours, than I would if you had a handsome face and wicked ways," Beauty assured him.

The Beast seemed pleased with this and sat back deep in thought. Beauty finished her supper, feeling almost comfortable in the Beast's company, until he suddenly said, "Beauty, will you marry me?"

Fear seized her heart. To refuse him might send him into a monstrous rage, but to accept was horrifying too, and she could not tell a lie. "I'm sorry, Beast, but no," she said, her voice shaking again, fearing that this night might, after all, be her last. Instead of a roar of anger the poor Beast merely sighed mournfully and said, "Then, goodnight, Beauty," and left the room, looking back at her again and again before he closed the door behind him.

Beauty listened to the mournful moans getting fainter as he made his way through the lavish lonely rooms of his palace. She went to bed feeling deeply sorry for the Beast. "How sad to appear so ugly, and be so good within."

And so the weeks and months passed. Every evening the Beast came to talk with her while she ate her supper. Every day, Beauty liked more and more things about him—his good common sense, his honesty and thoughtfulness. In every book she selected from the vast bookcases she always found a special little note for her, beautifully written in gold. She looked forward to his visits, and often arrived early at the table, waiting impatiently for the clock to strike nine. She now welcomed the creak of the stair and his shadow in the firelight.

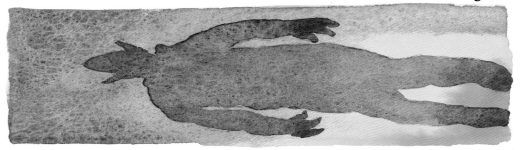

The one thing Beauty dreaded was the final topic of their conversations. Before leaving, he always asked her to marry him and she couldn't bear his sadness each time she refused him. "You upset me when you talk like this, Beast," she said one evening. "I hate to see you so sad but I can never marry you. I shall always be your friend. You must try to be content with that."

"I am indeed a very lucky Beast to have you as my friend. I am very ugly, I know, but I love you so much and if you would promise never to leave me, my happiness would be complete."

"That I can promise," said Beauty, "but you must allow me to visit my father. I have seen in the glass of the bookcase that he is ill with worrying about me. I think I will die with grief if you don't let me go to him."

"I don't want to cause you pain, Beauty," said the Beast. " I will send you home to see your father, but I am afraid that once you are there, you may never return to me. You have my heart, without you I would die."

"Oh, no!" cried Beauty. "I promise I will come back in seven days."

"Very well," said the Beast. "You shall be there tomorrow morning. All you need to do when you want to come back to me is to place this ring on the table beside you when you go to bed. Goodbye Beauty." Then he walked slowly from the room and closed the door behind him, leaving behind a small golden ring.

Beauty went to bed feeling deeply agitated. She felt guilty to have caused such anguish to her Beast yet hoped expectantly she might soon see her father again. When she woke up next morning she found herself in her old room in her father's house. Beside her bed was a trunk full of beautiful dresses. The Beast thought of everything. She put on the least showy of the dresses and ran to her father's room. He kissed and hugged his daughter again and again, he was so relieved to see her safe and sound. He called for her sisters and brothers. The brothers arrived first, brimming with joy at Beauty's return. Her sisters were slow in coming because they had found the trunk of fine dresses, and were feeling ill with jealousy. When Beauty tried to give them some of the dresses, the trunk and all of its contents vanished.

"It seems the Beast wants you to keep them all," said her father. "He must be very fond of you." With a flash, the trunk and dresses reappeared. And so Beauty told them about her life with the Beast, and of her promise she had made to return to him in seven days.

While Beauty's father and brothers showed her all the work they had been doing on the farm, her sisters plotted against her. "Why should she have so much, when we have so little. If we can keep her here for more than seven days, perhaps her Beast will get so angry he will gobble her up!"

For the rest of the week they smothered Beauty with hugs and kisses. When the seven days were up, they used the old onion trick again and, appearing completely heartbroken, begged her not to go. So Beauty agreed to stay for one more week. But on the tenth night, Beauty dreamed that she was back in the garden of the palace with the Beast lying at her feet close to death. She woke suddenly, shocked and ashamed. She, who never told a lie, had broken her promise to one who had showed her nothing but love and kindness. She immediately laid her ring on the table beside the bed, and fell asleep at once.

When she woke up, she was in her bed in the Beast's palace. She dressed herself in the most beautiful of all the gowns he had given her, but of the Beast there was no sign. She heard the clock strike the hours slowly through the day, and was seated at the table long before nine o'clock. The clock struck nine, but still the Beast did not appear. Beauty felt sick with concern as she ran through the palace, through distant towers and turrets she had never entered before, calling for him. She was close to despair when suddenly she remembered her dream. Rushing outside into the garden, she found him laying by her favorite rose bush.

Forgetting his ugliness, she threw herself upon him, her tear streaked cheek pressed against the deathly cold cheek of the Beast. She felt a slight slow heartbeat in his chest, and bathed his face with water from the stream. At last, the Beast opened his eyes and gasped, "You did not keep your promise to me. When you didn't return, I couldn't eat and my heart broke. Now I am dying."

"No, Beast! Don't die! Live and marry me! I thought I felt only friendship for you, but now I know it is love. We cannot live without each other." As soon as she said that, the moon burst through the clouds, and shooting stars and fiery comets criss-crossed the sky like a heavenly firework display. Beauty noticed nothing of this because her Beast had vanished. In his place lay a handsome stranger, a prince, who had been released from a wicked spell by Beauty's love.

"But where is my Beast?" cried Beauty.

"Your Beast is here, before you," said the prince. "Only you, in the whole world, saw my true self under my monstrous shape. You deserve far more than the golden crown I offer you."

"A heart of gold is more than enough for me," said Beauty, and they walked under the moon and the star-bursting sky. At the palace, as if by magic they found Beauty's entire family there to share their happiness. The palace was now alive with servants and musicians. Beauty's marriage to the prince was all that a father could wish for his daughter. Of course, Beauty's sisters were still jealous of her, but each found suitors at the grand wedding party and made better marriages than they deserved. Her brothers looked after the prince's estates and Beauty lived a life of great happiness surrounded by her family, and her beloved 'Beast.'

"At dawn and dusk Cormoran would
wade ashore and stalk through
the surrounding farmland…"

Jack THE Giant Killer

Long, long, long ago, at the far end of faraway Cornwall, lived a giant and his wife. His name was Cormoran, and his wife was called Cormelian. In those distant times, much of the land was covered in dense forest, and although he was the biggest and strongest giant in the land, Cormoran was fearful that the Cornish peasants would get so angry with him for stealing and gobbling up their cattle, that they might band together and creep up on him through the forest and try to kill him and his wife while they slept.

He decided to build a great hill of boulders so high that he could see over the forest. He would build a castle on top with windows which he could see through even when he and Cormelian were lying in their massive bed. And to make his castle even more secure, he would build his hill and castle some way out to sea.

Now, although Cormoran was huge and strong, he also thought that housework was woman's work. A castle, he reasoned, was really just a big house, so castle work must also be woman's work.

No sooner had the idea come to him than he set Cormelian the task of collecting the biggest granite boulders she could find. Then she had to carry the huge rocks out into the sea so that a mountain slowly rose from the seabed. Only when a rock proved too heavy even for the giantess to lift, did he lend a hand. But most of the time he sat on the ever-growing mount clutching his huge club and watching for any approaching horde of peasants.

At dawn and dusk Cormoran would wade ashore and stalk through the surrounding farmland, grabbing sheep by the handful and stuffing them into his sailcloth bag. He would tie cow's tails together and hang them three or four at a time over his shoulder.

The local peasants were in despair. Winter was approaching and they knew they and their children would face near starvation when the storms stopped them fishing, and Cormoran continued to devour their cattle. They must get rid of the giant . . . but how?

Things were about to get even worse for the local people. Now, as well as being enormous and very strong, most giants can perform bits and pieces of magic. Just little things, from time to time. Well, Cormoran had been very clever; he had saved up all his scraps of magic for months and months and was determined to use them all up in one great spell.

He sat on his island of rocks and tensed all his muscles, clenched his great fists, gritted his horrible teeth, screwed up his eyes and grunted and groaned and BANG! From the sky above his head came a thunderclap so loud it shook houses and cottages all the way to Land's End.

As frightened villagers ran out of their homes, there it was—on top of the mount of rocks—a castle! Cormoran had magicked a castle out of thin air. A gigantic giant's castle complete with turrets and windows and battlements from which Cormoran could aim his slingshot at any foe.

"We can't attack him now," wailed the villagers. "We need an expert," said one of the village elders, "we need a professional giant killer."

Poor though they were, the people of the surrounding farms and villages collected together all the odd coin and silver trinkets and gold teeth they had hidden for a rainy day, and offered them in a leather bag to anyone brave enough to attempt to rid them of the giants.

News of the prize spread the whole length of Cornwall and beyond, but no one, when they had seen the formidable castle and the size of Cormoran and his wife, no one came forward to accept the challenge. Except one; a boy called Jack, who lived with his mother and father in a cottage high up on the moors.

The news of the giants and their castle and the bag of prize money had been slow to reach their remote cottage, and Jack was anxious to get down to the seashore to see for himself. His parents begged him not to go, but Jack was determined—and he had a plan!

When Jack arrived that evening, the seashore was cloaked in a thick sea mist. The top of Cormoran's castle was just visible against the darkening sky, but all below was hidden from view.

"Perfect," muttered Jack to himself, "just the job." And he began to dig. He dug for many hours. Deeper and deeper into the sandy beach. He had a rope secured to a rock on the surface and when he thought his pit deep enough, he climbed up the rope and covered the top of the pit with thin planks of wood. Finally, he spread sand over the planks so no trace of the deep pit remained. And he sat himself down and watched the warmth of dawn disperse the sea mist.

"Ahoy! Lord Cormoran!" shouted Jack standing on a rock and waving an axe in the air. "Wakey! Wakey!" All the villagers, hiding along the cliff tops were amazed at Jack's bravery, although some were worried that he would just make the giants angry and they would all suffer.

But in the castle high on the Mount, the giant's snoring drowned even the sound of the pounding waves. Jack's little voice had no more effect than the constant scream of the gulls. Then Cormoran's stomach rumbled.

"Wife," he grumbled, poking the sleeping Cormelian in the ribs. "Wife. Where's my breakfast?"

"Fetch it yourself," she growled in reply. "You couldn't be bothered to steal any cattle last night because it was foggy, so you will have to go and pick up a few now."

"Bah!" cursed Cormoran, and stumped out of bed and threw open the great door of the castle. He was in a filthy mood and hungry. Someone was going to suffer today; he snatched up his mighty club, as big as an oak tree, and glared towards the shore.

"What's that speck dancing up and down on that rock?" he muttered to himself. "Why, he is waving at me, the cheeky little devil. He'll be my first snack of the morning while I look for something more substantial." And Cormoran leapt into the sea and with one, two, three strides was almost at the shore.

Instead of running away, Jack skipped about on his rock and even blew a blast on the horn he had slung across his shoulder. This so enraged Cormoran that he raised his club and rushed up the beach to squash this tiny human fly. The beach gave way beneath him and the sides of the pit caved in around him, leaving only his ugly head sticking out. Quick as a flash, with a chop, chop, chop, Jack sent the head rolling back down the beach and into the waves.

Jack heard the sound of cheering from the cliff tops, and turned to wave at the villagers only to see them all duck down again. A terrible scream came from the castle on the Mount, and there was the giant's wife advancing towards them.

Jack turned to run, but then noticed that the giantess seemed to be getting smaller as she charged through the waves. "Yes," Jack gasped to himself, "she is shrinking."

Only magic had kept her and her husband so huge, and with his death, the spell was getting weaker and weaker. The sea was now up to her waist, and now her shoulders. With flailing arms, she managed to reach shallow water but was now no larger than a little girl, and now a cat ... and now a mouse. At that moment a seagull swooped down, snatched up the teeny giantess and flew off, back to the castle on the Mount. No one ever saw her again.

So, young Jack was cheered and carried shoulder high through the narrow streets, and presented with the bag of coin, silver and gold.

"We are all poor people," Jack said, "you can't afford to give me such a prize. Please keep your money."

The poor people of Cornwall cheered even more loudly, and insisted that Jack and his parents come to live in the great castle on the Mount. And there they lived for many happy years. Jack sometimes fancied, late at night, that he heard a scurrying and scratching around the pantry or in the kitchen, and wondered if it could be the teeny giantess fighting off the mice for a few scraps of food.

He never laid traps and never had a cat, just in case poor little Cormelian got caught. And he always made sure there were a few tasty leftovers from supper under the kitchen table.

After all, she had built the great castle and it stands on its high rocky island in Mount's Bay to this day.

"So Little Red Riding Hood set off to the next village to visit her grandmother."

LITTLE RED *Riding Hood*

Once upon a time, by the edge of a deep, dark wood, there lived a little girl. Her mother adored her and her grandmother, who lived in the next village, adored her even more. Grandmother made the little girl a red hood like the ones fine ladies wear when they go riding. The child loved the hood so much that she wore it every day and soon everybody was calling her Little Red Riding Hood.

One day her mother baked some cakes on the griddle and said "Little Red Riding Hood, your granny is sick; take her these cakes and a bottle of wine. It will cheer her up."

So Little Red Riding Hood set off to the next village to visit her grandmother. As she walked through the wood she met a wolf who, being a wolf, wanted to eat her up but did not dare to because there were woodcutters working nearby.

"Where are you going, little girl?" the wolf asked, smiling sweetly.

The child did not know how dangerous it was to talk to strangers,

particularly wolves, and replied, "To my grandmother, Mr. Wolf, and I have cakes and wine to cheer her up."

And where does your grandmother live, child?" asked the wolf.

"Oh, she lives beyond the wood, near the old mill," replied Little Red Riding Hood.

The wolf thought to himself, "What a tender young creature! She would make a plump and tasty meal—she would be better to eat than the old woman, I'm sure, but if I am crafty, I can eat both of them."

The wolf smiled another big toothy smile. "My child," he said, "cakes and wine are all very well, but what grannies really, really love are flowers. Look around you, the wood is full of wonderful flowers. Take a bunch to your old grandmother."

Little Red Riding Hood looked around, and it was true; the wood was carpeted with a blue haze of bluebells. "Good idea, Mr. Wolf. Thank you, Mr. Wolf," and Red Riding Hood began to pick the flowers. While the little girl gathered bluebells, the wolf ran the shortest path to grandmother's house and knocked on the door.

"Who is there?" called Grandmother from inside. The wolf put on his best high, girly voice.

"Lift up the latch and walk right in," called Grandmother. The wolf lifted the latch, and without saying a word he went straight to grandmother's bed and gobbled her up. Then he put on her clothes, put on her cap, drew the curtains and lay down in bed.

Red Riding Hood knocked on the door and heard a croaky voice say, "Who's there?"

"Poor Grandmother," she thought, "she sounds very sick."

"Red Riding Hood, Granny. I've come to cheer you up."

"Lift the latch and come right in, my dear," croaked the wolf, trying to pull the cap down further over his ears. Little Red Riding Hood lifted the latch and stepped into the dark room.

"Oh! Granny," Red Riding Hood said as she pulled the curtains, "What big ears you have."

"All the better to hear you with, my child," came the reply. Little Red Riding Hood stepped closer to the figure in the bed.

"But, Grandmother, what big eyes you have."

"All the better to see you with, my dear." said the wolf, trying to smile sweetly.

"Oh! But Grandmother, what big teeth you have!"

"All the better to eat you with!" said the wolf and leapt upon Little Red Riding Hood and swallowed her, whole.

Then he lay down on the bed, patted his big, fat stomach and fell fast asleep and began to snore very loudly.

A little while later, a woodcutter on his way to work passed by grandmother's cottage and was surprised by the sound of snoring. "I've never heard the old lady make such a racket," thought a woodcutter. "I must see if she is alright." And in he went and found the wolf wearing grandmother's clothes and sleeping on her bed.

"You old rogue," thought the woodcutter and he was about to chop the wolf in two when he thought the grandmother might still be saved. With his sharpest saw he carefully cut open the fat stomach of the sleeping wolf and out sprang Red Riding Hood followed by Grandmother who was most upset that the woodcutter saw her in her underwear.

Then they filled the wolf up with heavy stones and grandmother sewed up his stomach. When the wolf woke up he was so heavy and slow he couldn't catch anyone ever again and became a vegetarian.

And Little Red Riding Hood was always very careful about speaking to strangers.

"...a prince out hunting, rode past the tower
and heard Rapunzel's beautiful song."

Rapunzel

Once upon a time there was a man and wife who longed to have a child. Then, at last, the wife began to feel that their wishes might be granted.

There was a little window at the back of their house, and through it they could see into their neighbors' garden. It was a beautiful garden, full of wonderful plants and flowers. It was surrounded by a high wall and no one dared to go in there because it belonged to an enchantress who had evil powers and was feared by all.

One day, the wife was looking from the little window into the garden where she saw an area given to the most beautiful rampion (rapunzel). It looked so fresh and green that she longed to taste it.

She longed and she longed for it, and became quite upset that what she craved was just out of reach. Her husband worried about her fretting so much, and when he heard of her desire he vowed to get enough rapunzel for a tasty salad.

In the evening twilight the man climbed over the wall into the enchantress' garden and grabbed a handful of rapunzel and hurried back to his wife. Swiftly she made a rapunzel salad with a little olive oil and wolfed it down. Delicious! So delicious that next day she wanted more.

Once again, the man waited til twilight and then climbed over the wall. This time he grabbed an armful of rapunzel plants but, as he turned to climb back over the wall, he found himself face to face with the dreaded enchantress.

"How dare you," she said, her eyes red with anger, "climb into my garden and steal my rapunzels? You shall suffer for it!"

"Oh! Please have mercy," begged the poor man. "I did it out of love for my wife who is to have a baby. My wife saw your rapunzels from our window and had such a powerful longing for them I feared she would die."

The red in the eyes of the enchantress cooled slightly.

"If what you say is true, I will let you take as much rapunzel as you wish, only make one condition. When your child is safely born you must give me whatever I wish."

The terrified man agreed, and there was nothing he owned that he would not give for the longed-for baby.

So the enchantress gave the man a key to her garden and allowed him to pick rapunzel whenever he wished. When the baby was born, the enchantress appeared immediately and demanded the man honor the agreement they had made.

"Yes," said the man, overjoyed that he and his wife at last had a lovely, healthy daughter. "I will give you whatever you want."

"I want your baby," said the enchantress, her eyes now as cold as ice. "I will call her Rapunzel, so you are paying me for my rapunzel with your Rapunzel."

"No!" cried the man, but the enchantress had already snatched the baby from its cradle, and vanished.

For weeks, and months after, the man and his wife watched, grief-stricken from their window but there was no sign of the enchantress and their baby daughter. The garden became overgrown and the patch of rapunzel withered and died.

Far away, in another part of the country, Rapunzel grew into the most beautiful girl under the sun. She became so beautiful, that the enchantress grew jealous and cast a spell which shut the girl away at the top of a high tower with no door and no stairs, and with only a small window under the roof. The tower was in the middle of a deep, dark forest and nobody ventured near.

Whenever the enchantress wanted to come in she stood below and called out:

"Rapunzel, Rapunzel.

Let down your hair to me."

Rapunzel had magnificent long golden hair as strong as could be and, when she heard the enchantress calling, she would unfasten the braided tresses, wrap them round a window-hook and then let her hair fall all the way to the ground. Then the enchantress would climb up it.

It was lonely for Rapunzel in her tower. Nobody entered the dark heart of the forest and her only companions were a family of swifts who made their nest near her high window. The birds sang to Rapunzel and she sang to the birds.

Then, after two or three years, a prince out hunting, rode past the tower and heard Rapunzel's beautiful song.

He looked for a door to the tower but none was to be found. He rode home, but the singing touched him deeply, and every day he returned to the forest to listen.

One day he saw the enchantress come and he heard how she called:

"Rapunzel, Rapunzel.

Let down your hair to me."

Then Rapunzel let down her hair and the enchantress climbed up to her.

"Well, if that's the golden ladder that you have to climb, I too will give it a try."

He waited until the enchantress had departed and, as it grew dark, he approached the tower and called:

"Rapunzel, Rapunzel.

Let down your hair to me."

Rapunzel was surprised that the enchantress had returned so soon, and the voice sounded rather different.

"She must be out of breath, having returned so swiftly," she decided, and sent her hair tumbling down to the darkening forest.

Hand over hand, with beating heart, the prince climbed the golden tresses. At first, Rapunzel was terribly frightened when a man came through her window for she had never seen such a sight before but, the prince spoke to her quietly and like a friend. He told her that his heart had been so touched by her singing that he couldn't rest without seeing her.

Slowly, Rapunzel lost her fear and, when the prince asked her if she would take him for her husband, and by now she liked what she saw of him, she thought, "He will treat me more kindly than that old godmother does." She laid her hand in his and said, "Yes. I would like to go away with you but, I don't know how to get down. Every time you come to visit, bring a thread of silk and I will weave a ladder with them. When it is ready, I will climb down and you can carry me off on your horse."

They agreed that he should come to her every evening, for the enchantress came by day and noticed nothing until Rapunzel absent-mindedly wondered, "Tell me, godmother, how it happens that you are so much heavier for me to pull up than the king's son? He is up in a moment."

"Ah! You wicked child!" cried the enchantress. "What's that you say? I thought I had hidden you forever from the wicked world and yet you have betrayed me."

In her rage she grabbed Rapunzel's tresses, wrapped them twice around her left hand and seized a pair of scissors with her right and snip, snap, cut off the lovely hair.

Then she took Rapunzel away into a wild desert and left her there to live in misery.

On the evening of the same day that she had cast out Rapunzel, the enchantress returned to the tower and fastened the braids of hair which she had cut off to the window. When the prince came and cried:

"Rapunzel, Rapunzel.

Let down your hair to me."

She let the hair down.

The prince climbed quickly up but, instead of finding his beautiful Rapunzel, he found the evil enchantress.

"Aha," she cried, enjoying his horror. "So you've come to collect your beautiful bird, have you? Well she's not in this nest any more, and she's not singing any more. The cat's got her and will scratch your eyes out as well. You will never see her again."

The prince was out of his mind with despair and leapt from the tower. He fell into bushes which broke his fall and, although he escaped with his life, thorns on the bushes pierced both of his eyes.

Then he wandered, blind, about the forest, eating only berries and roots and weeping over his lost love. In his misery he roamed for some years until he came to the desert where Rapunzel lived in great distress and where she had given birth to twins, a boy and a girl.

He heard a song, sad yet so familiar that he was drawn toward it. Rapunzel recognized him and hugged him and wept, pressing her cheek to his. Two of her tears fell upon his eyes and they cleared and he could see again. He could see his beautiful Rapunzel and their children.

So he took Rapunzel and their children home to his kingdom where they were welcomed with great joy, and they lived for a long time, happy and contented.

In a far away garden, rapunzel suddenly grew once more below the window of a man and his wife. The man still had the key to the enchantress's garden and he unlocked the gate so that his children could play there. After the loss of their first born they had been blessed with three more children, and when they played in the overgrown garden, it became beautiful once more.

*"He had a different outfit for
every hour of the day…"*

THE *Emperor's* NEW *Clothes*

 Many, many years ago there was an Emperor who was so terribly fond of smart new clothes that he spent all his money on his fancy fashions. He did not care about visiting his army or his navy, or going to the theater, or even going for a ride in the park. Unless of course, it gave him an opportunity to show off his new clothes. He had a different outfit for every hour of the day; and just as they say of a king, "He is in his council chamber," the Emperor's subjects used to say, "He is in his clothes closet."

Life at the court was always merry and gay, and visitors came from far and wide. One day, two rogues calling themselves weavers, arrived. They said they could weave the most wonderful cloth; the finest stuff in the most beautiful colors and the most elaborate patterns. Not only that, but the cloth had the strange quality of being invisible to anyone who was unfit for his job, or who was really stupid.

"These would be truly marvelous clothes!" cried the Emperor. "Why, if I had such a wondrous outfit, I could tell immediately which

of my subjects were doing to their jobs properly and I could pick out the wise from the foolish! You must weave some material for me, and I don't care what it costs!"

He gave the rogues a great deal of money so they could start working at once. The rogues set up two looms and acted as if they were weaving, but they had nothing at all on their looms. All the gold threads and fine silks they demanded from the Emperor they did not use, but hid them in their own backpacks. They sat at their looms late into the night pretending to weave the wondrous cloth.

The Emperor was impatient to see how the work was progressing, but he remembered that anyone unworthy of his job or who was really stupid, would not be able to see the cloth. He was not really worried that this would happen to him; but it might be better to send someone else to see how the weavers were doing.

"I will send my faithful old Prime Minister for he is both wise and very experienced in his position."

So, the old Prime Minister went to the hall where the rogues were pretending to be hard at work. He opened his eyes wide but could see nothing on the looms. He opened his eyes even wider, but still he could see nothing. The cheating weavers invited the old Prime Minister to step closer so that he might admire the fine detail of the pattern and the glorious color of the cloth. The old minister went closer, cleaned the spectacles on the end of his nose, and peered intently at the looms.

"Am I stupid?" he thought to himself, "am I too stupid for my job? I can't believe it, but if it is so, it is best no one finds out about it."

"Tell us, Prime Minister, what do you think of it?"

"The color is glorious," mumbled the old Prime Minister, "and the pattern is indeed very fine. I shall tell the Emperor how very beautiful I think them."

"We are most obliged, Prime Minister," said the rogues, "and do describe to the Emperor how well the orange color blends with the pink, and how the little blue flowers spell out his name." Then they asked for more fine silk and gold thread so that they might finish their work.

The Emperor was delighted with the Prime Minister's description of the glowing colors and was thrilled to learn that the cloth bore his name, spelled out in tiny blue flowers. The Emperor was now even more impatient and sent the Minister for the Arts to enquire how quickly the cloth could be finished. Just like the Prime Minister, he looked and looked; but all he could see were empty looms.

"Does the material look as wonderful to you as it did to your Lord, the Prime Minister?" asked one of the rogues.

"Surely, I'm not stupid," thought the Minister of the Arts, "and am I not worth all the money I am paid? I can't have anyone think that." And so he praised the color and the pattern and the wonderful richness of the cloth, and reported back to the Emperor about the cloth he could not see.

"Truly, your Imperial Majesty, the work of the weavers is extraordinarily magnificent."

By now everyone in the city had heard of the cloth's amazing quality and all were curious to see how stupid their neighbors were. The Emperor himself wished to see the costly material immediately, even while it was still on the loom. Attended by the most important lords and ladies in the Empire, including the Prime Minister and the Minister for the Arts who had been there before, the Emperor entered the hall where the weavers were still pretending to be hard at work.

"Isn't it magnificent?" asked the Prime Minister. "Your Majesty, see the glorious colors and patterns," said the Minister for the Arts. And both Ministers pointed to the empty looms, believing everyone else could see the amazing cloth.

The Emperor felt rather nervous. He couldn't see anything on the looms, no matter how hard he tried.

"What's this?" thought the Emperor, "they can see it and I can't. Am I stupid? Am I not fit to be an Emperor? That would be the most dreadful thing." And then he said aloud, "Oh! How pretty! Charming! Excellent. It has our esteemed approval."

A murmur of appreciation from the assembled lords and ladies grew into a roar of exaltation as they competed with one another in praise of the cloth which none of them could see.

"Truly lovely! So pretty! Gorgeous, your Majesty!"

They advised the Emperor to have the clothes cut and sewn ready for the next big procession, so that all his people could admire him in what would be his most splendid outfit ever. The Emperor was so delighted that he ordered that the two weavers be given the title "Imperial Knights of the Loom."

The two rogues sat up the whole night before the day of the procession. They had sixteen lamps lighting up the room and crowds peered through the window to see how busy they were finishing the Emperor's new clothes. They pretended to take the cloth from the loom; they made cuts in the air with their big scissors, and sewed with needles without thread. At the first pink light of dawn, they cried, "See! The Emperor's new clothes are ready!" And the crowds outside in the street cheered.

The Emperor came with all his courtiers; and the cheats lifted their arms as if they were holding something, and one said "Behold, your Majesty's trousers! This is the robe and here is the long train. All as light as spider webs. It will feel as if your Majesty had nothing on, but that is just the beauty of this delicate cloth."

Yes, indeed!" said all the courtiers, although not one of them could see anything, for nothing was there. The Minister for the Arts was particularly fulsome with his praises. "Surely nothing, nothing in the entire history of our country, has been quite so extraordinarily beautiful."

"If your Imperial Majesty will be graciously pleased to take off his clothes," said the rogues, "we will fit on the new outfit, here in front of the mirror."

"How splendid his Majesty looks in his new clothes!" everyone cried out. "What colors! What a pattern. How well it fits!"

"And see the little blue flowers!" exclaimed the Prime Minister.

"Why, yes!" went up the cry, "see the little blue flowers!"

"Your Majesty, the crimson canopy which is to be held above your head in the procession is awaiting you outside."

The Emperor took off all his clothes, and the rogues acted as if they were handing him each piece of his new clothing.

The Emperor turned and twisted in front of the mirror.

The two Lords of the Imperial Bedchamber, who were supposed to carry the Emperor's train, stooped down just as if they were picking up the robe and held their hands as if they were carrying it.

So, the Emperor walked under his crimson canopy in the procession through the streets of his city. The crowds cried out, "Oh! How beautiful are our Emperor's new clothes," and, "How well they fit him." None of them could admit that they could see nothing, for their neighbors would think they must be stupid or unfit for the jobs they held.

Never before had the Emperor's clothes been such a success with all his people. Except one. A little boy, sitting on his father's shoulders, cried out, "But he doesn't have any clothes on!"

"What did he say?" asked the people round about.

"He said the Emperor has no clothes on," said the child's father proudly. And what the innocent child had said was whispered from one to another. "The little boy says the Emperor doesn't have anything on."

And, at last, the crowd cried out "But he's right! The Emperor has nothing on at all!"

The Emperor was dismayed, for he realized that the people were right; but he was the Emperor and the procession must go on, so he walked on, head held hight, all the way back to his palace. And the lords of the bedchamber went on pretending to carry the train that wasn't there, and the Ministers wished they had been as honest as the little boy.

The two rogues had already left the country; on the lookout, no doubt, for more vain people with more money than sense.

"...there, in the rain, stood a girl
soaked from head to foot."

THE Princess AND THE Pea

Once upon a time there was a prince who wanted to marry a princess. But not just any princess. There were plenty of princesses but not one of them was quite right. He asked all his most trusted courtiers, "How can I find the right princess, one who is a true princess right to the very tips of her toes?" One suggested a test of intelligence, another to examine the quality of tailoring in her dresses—yet another the styles of their hair! But the prince remained unconvinced. There must be a way to tell the true, good-hearted princesses from the pretenders, he thought.

He travelled all over the world looking for the perfect one, but returned home sad and disappointed. One evening a fierce storm broke over the kingdom. Lightning flashed and thunder boomed and rain poured down. The whole palace had been trapped indoors for most of the day—very bored. The prince had gone to bed to read a good book, but his mother, the old queen, stayed up sewing. Some of the stitches were a bit uneven where a particularly noisy thunderclap had made her jump!

Suddenly, between the claps of thunder, a loud knock was heard on the castle gate. The old queen sent her butler to see who on earth could be calling at this time of night. The butler, rather flustered, rushed out to answer the knocking. When he swung the great gate open, there, in the rain, stood a girl, soaked from head to foot. Water streamed down her hair and her clothes. "I am Princess Louisa!" she shouted above the patter of raindrops. "I was out for a walk this evening and got caught in the storm. Perhaps I could take shelter here for the night?"

She didn't look much like a princess, but the kind old butler couldn't leave her out there in such horrible weather. He invited her into the grand hall of the castle and, feeling rather flustered, introduced her to the queen who told her to sit before the fire.

She looks more like a drowned rat, thought the old queen, but we'll find out if she is a real princess quickly enough. Aware of her son's fruitless search for a true princess, she had devised her own test which she was sure would work. She hurried to the guest room and took all the bedclothes off the bed; then on the bare bedstead she put a dried pea. On top of the pea she put twenty mattresses; and on top of the mattresses she put twenty eiderdown quilts, nice and soft and squishy. That was the bed on which the princess had to sleep.

The queen rushed back down to where the princess was slowly but surely drying off by the fire. "Your bed is ready for the night," she said. "We like to make guests comfortable."

When the princess saw the bed she was to sleep on, she could hardly believe her luck! Why, she was going to have the best night's sleep ever!

"Thank you, it's very kind of you," the princess said. "I'm sure I shall sleep very well in that."

"We'll see," the queen thought to herself, but all she said was, "Good night."

The princess changed out of her wet clothes and into the night-gown that had been laid out for her. She was feeling very sleepy. She climbed up to the top of the twenty mattresses and eiderdowns and flopped, exhausted, into bed. She closed her eyes gratefully, ready to fall asleep. But no matter how much she wriggled around trying to get

comfortable, she couldn't! She tossed and turned, having the most dreadful time. After a while she thought she must be going mad. It felt as if there was something small and hard pressing into her back. Surely all these soft eiderdowns and mattresses should make it the most comfy place in the world to sleep!

Next morning, when the old queen asked her how she had slept, she felt a bit nervous. After all the queen's kind hospitality, should she admit what had really happened? She didn't want to offend her, but she didn't like to lie either. So she replied, "Terribly, I'm afraid. I hardly slept a wink. I know it sounds silly, and I don't know what was in that bed, but it felt as if there was something hard under the mattresses. It kept me awake all night long."

The old queen smiled. "Come along, my dear, and have some breakfast." Now they knew she was a real princess, since she had felt the pea through twenty mattresses and twenty eiderdown quilts. She was sure that only a real princess could be so sensitive!

When the prince came down to breakfast that morning, he was rather surprised to find a beautiful stranger at the table. When his mother told him all about the test, and that she had found him a true princess, he was delighted. He fell in love with her almost instantly—and she was just as sensitive, true and kind-hearted as the test had shown. So the prince married the princess, and the pea was exhibited in the royal museum. You can go there and see it, if you don't believe me.

"And there, in the heart of the flower sat a tiny girl."

Thumbelina

Once upon a time there was a woman who longed to have a little child. Because she had no idea how to get one, she went to an old woman who lived near the woods who did spells and knew many strange things.

"I would so love to have a little child. Please could you tell me where I can get one?"

"Oh, that's not so difficult," replied the old woman, who was probably a witch. "Take this grain of barley; it's not the kind that farmers grow or that you feed your chickens. Plant it in a flowerpot, and you shall see what you shall see."

"Thank you," said the woman and handed over twelve pennies for the grain of barley and rushed off home to plant it. No sooner had she pushed the grain into the soil than it started to sprout. It quickly grew into a big beautiful flower, shaped like a tulip with tightly closed petals of red and yellow.

"Oh, it's so beautiful," cried the woman and kissed it. One by one the petals slowly parted and opened into a wonderful bloom. And there, in the heart of the flower sat a tiny girl. She was slightly smaller than the woman's thumb so she called the little child Thumbelina.

A polished shell of a walnut became Thumbelina's cradle, blue violet petals were her mattress, and a rose petal her coverlet. There she slept at night; in the daytime she played on the table by the window, where the woman had placed a bowl of water with a garland of flowers around it. In this tiny "lake" there floated a green tulip leaf and on this Thumbelina could sit and row from one side of the plate to the other, with two white horsehairs for oars. And while she sailed she sang in a high, delicate voice.

One night, as Thumbelina lay sleeping in her little bed, an old toad crept through a broken pane in the window. Old toad was wet and slimy and hopped down onto the table and peered at the tiny girl.

"That would be a lovely wife for my son," thought the toad and picked up the walnut shell in which Thumbelina slept and hopped back down into the garden.

On the bank of a broad stream, just where it was most muddy, lived the old toad and her son. He was as ugly as his mother and, "croak, croak, croak," was all he said when he saw Thumbelina.

"Shhh! Not so loud," scolded his mother, "or she will wake and run away. We will put her on one of the broad water lily leaves in the middle of the stream. It will be like an island for her. Then she can't get away while we get our house ready for the wedding."

Out in the center of the stream grew many water lilies. The biggest leaf was furthest from the bank and to that the old toad swam and laid Thumbelina's little bed.

When the tiny girl woke in the morning and saw that she was stranded on a leaf with water all around, she cried and cried. She could see no way of getting to shore. The old toad was busy down in her muddy house, decorating the rooms with yellow weed and rushes. Then she swam out with her ugly son to collect Thumbelina's bed.

"This is my son, Toady," the old toad said. "He will be your husband and you will live happily down in the lovely mud." Then they swam away with the little bed to put it in their best room; but Thumbelina sat all alone on the lily leaf and wept.

The little fishes swimming in the water below had seen the toads and heard what had been said. They popped their heads out of the water and peered over the ides of the leaf to see the tiny girl.

"So beautiful! So beautiful," they burbled and it hurt them to think she would have to marry a toad so they began to nibble through the stalk that held the leaf anchored to the bottom of the stream. Suddenly the leaf was free and drifted away bearing Thumbelina far from Toady and his mother.

The little birds and trees along the shore sang "What a lovely little girl," as Thumbelina sailed past. Farther and farther sailed the leaf, past towns and cities, taking her on a journey to foreign lands.

A white butterfly fluttered around her and kept her company, and then finally landed on the water lily leaf. Thumbelina took a silk ribbon from around her waist and tied one end of it to the butterfly and the other end to the leaf. Pulled by the butterfly, the leaf glided on much faster.

Then, when Thumbelina was really enjoying the ride, a big May bug flew down and snatched the little girl around her waist and

carried her off, up into the trees. The water lily leaf floated on down the stream and the butterfly had to go with it. As terrified as she was by the May bug, Thumbelina was even more concerned for the poor butterfly, chained by her ribbon to follow the leaf.

The May bug didn't care about the butterfly. He cared only for this beautiful, tiny girl. He perched her on the biggest leaf on the tree and gave her fresh honey to eat, and told her she was the loveliest thing he had ever seen, even though she didn't look much like a May bug.

Soon all the other May bugs in the area came to visit and inspect the newcomer. One young lady May bug said, "Why, she has no more than two legs. How strange is that?" Another cried, "She has no feelers!" and yet another said, "Disgusting! She has such a thin waist, she looks like a human being! How ugly!"

All the other lady bugs agreed with them. The May bug who had caught Thumbelina, and who still thought her pretty, gradually began to change his mind. If everyone thought her ugly, then he didn't want her any longer. He flew Thumbelina down to the ground and left her there.

Poor Thumbelina cried, "How ugly I must be that even a May bug doesn't want me."

All through that summer, Thumbelina lived alone in the forest. She made a little hammock out of grass and hung it beneath a dock leaf for shade and to protect her from rain while she slept. She ate the honey from the flowers and drank the dew from the leaves.

Summer and autumn passed and then came the sharp cold of winter. Birds flew away and leaves fell from the trees, flowers withered and the dock leaf shrivelled and crumbled until nothing remained but the stalk. Thumbelina was terribly cold. Her clothes were tattered and, without shelter, she would surely freeze to death.

Now, at the edge of the forest was a great corn field, but the corn had been harvested long ago, only a few patches of stubble stood in the frozen ground. To Thumbelina these stubble stalks were like another forest and she wandered amongst them seeking shelter from the winter wind. Then she arrived at the entrance of a field mouse's home. It was just a little hole under the stubble. But deep down below, the field mouse lived warm and snug, and had a whole store room of nuts and corn and dried fruit.

Thumbelina stood like a little beggar girl and asked for a single grain of barley corn for she had not eaten for two days.

"You poor little soul," said the field mouse—for she was a good old

friendly field mouse—come into the warm and dine with me." The field mouse liked Thumbelina instantly and said, "You can stay all winter if you keep the place tidy and tell me a story every day." Thumbelina agreed.

"Soon we shall have a visitor," continued the field mouse. "Once a week my neighbor comes to visit me. He has an even grander home than mine, and a beautiful black fur coat. If you could persuade him to be your husband you would be very well looked after. You must tell the prettiest stories you know."

When the visitor arrived, Thumbelina did not think she would ever wish to marry him, despite his velvety black fur coat, for he was a mole. The field mouse spoke of how rich he was and how his home was twenty times larger than hers, and that he was cultured and very learned but did not like sunlight which hurt his eyes, and he had never seen flowers. In fact, he could barely see anything, but he fell in love with Thumbelina when the field mouse asked her to sing for him.

He had dug a tunnel from his house to theirs, and invited Thumbelina and the field mouse to use it as often as they pleased. He warned them not to be afraid of the dead bird which was lying in the passage. It must have died very recently after seeking shelter.

When they came to where the dead bird lay, the mole pushed his broad nose against the ceiling, so that a hole was made and the daylight could shine down. The bird was a swallow, his beautiful wings pressed tight against his sides, and his head and feet drawn back under his feathers. Thumbelina felt a great sadness for she loved all the birds who had sung for her that summer. The mole kicked the bird with one of his stubby little legs and said, "Now it doesn't chirp any more. It must be miserable to be born a bird. I am thankful none of my children will be born birds! All birds can do is chirp, chirp, and die of hunger when winter comes."

"Well, of course you are right as usual," said the field mouse. "Oh what use is all that tweet, tweet when winter comes?"

Thumbelina didn't say a word, but when the mouse and mole had their backs turned, she pushed aside the feathers which covered the bird's head and kissed the closed eye of the swallow.

"Perhaps you were one of the birds that sang so sweetly for me in the summer," she thought. And she kissed his eye again.

The mole closed up the hole through which the daylight shone, and escorted the ladies back to their home. That night Thumbelina could not sleep so she got up and wove a coverlet of hay and dragged it down the dark passage and covered the bird with it. She tucked dry leaves and thistledown under the bird's sides to protect him from the cold earth.

"Farewell, beautiful bird," she said, "farewell, and thank you for your summer song."

She put her head on the bird's breast; and then gasped and jumped up! Thump. Thump. It was the bird's heart, for the swallow was not completely dead and now the warmth had revived it.

Thumbelina trembled, for the bird was far larger than her. But she was a brave little child and she pressed thistledown closer around the bird, and brought her own coverlet and laid it over the bird's head.

The next night she crept down the dark passage again; the swallow was a little better but still very weak. He opened his eyes just enough to see Thumbelina standing in the dark.

"Thank you, sweet child," said the sick swallow. "I'm feeling much better. I am not cold now. Soon I shall be strong enough to fly out into the sunshine."

"Oh no!" she said. "It's so cold and snowing outside now. You would freeze. Stay here in your warm bed, and I will nurse you." Then she brought the swallow water in a nutshell; and the swallow drank and told her how he had torn his wing on a thorn bush and could not fly as fast as the other swallows on their flight to the warm countries. Winter had caught up with him and he had fainted from the cold and fallen to earth. He could remember nothing more and did not know how he came to be in the mole's passageway.

The swallow stayed all winter, and Thumbelina took good care of him and told the field mouse and mole nothing about it because she knew they didn't like the poor swallow.

As soon as spring came, and the sun warmed the earth, the swallow opened up the hole in the ceiling which the mole had made. The sun shone in upon them.

"Come with me, Thumbelina," the swallow said. "Sit upon my back and we will fly to the greenwood."

"No, I cannot," said Thumbelina, "the old field mouse will be sad and lonely if I leave." The swallow thanked her again and called,

"Farewell, farewell, lovely girl." And flew out into the sunshine.

Soon the corn in the field above grew high and it was quite a forest for the tiny girl.

"You must spend this summer preparing for your wedding," said the field mouse, "for my neighbor, Mr. Mole, wants to marry you soon. What good fortune for a poor child like you! Now you must work at your outfit and make woollen and linen clothes for when you become Mrs. Mole."

Thumbelina had to spin and the field mouse hired four spiders to weave both day and night. Every evening the mole came to visit, saying how much he hated the sun which baked the earth so hard that it was difficult to dig in. As soon as autumn came they would be married. Thumbelina was not happy; she thought the mole was dull and she did not love him. Every day, at sunrise and sunset, she crept to the entrance of her dark home, and when the breeze blew the corn ears apart so that she could see the sky, she thought how light and beautiful it was out there, and longed to see her dear swallow again.

Then the corn was cut and autumn came. "In four weeks we shall hold your wedding," said the field mouse, and Thumbelina wept and said she didn't want to be Mrs. Mole.

"Nonsense, cried the field mouse, "don't be silly. He will be an excellent husband, he has a kitchen and a larder, both full, and a fur coat which is finer than any coat in the queen's wardrobe."

The day of the wedding arrived, and the mole came to fetch

Thumbelina. She was to live in his house deep under the ground. Once there, she felt she might never see the sun again.

"Farewell, beautiful sun," she said and lifted her arms to the sky and took a few steps out onto the field. The harvest was over and only the stubble was left. She saw one little red flower as tall as her head. She hugged the flower and said, "Good-bye. And give my love to the swallow if he should pass this way."

"Tweet, tweet," She looked up and the swallow swooped down from the sky and landed beside her. "I've been waiting to ask you one last time to fly away with me," he said. "Come to the warmest countries before the winter catches me again."

This time Thumbelina did not hesitate. She climbed onto the swallow's back. She tied herself with a ribbon to one of the bird's feathers; then the swallow flew up and over the forest and over the sea, high up over great mountains where there is always snow. She hid under the bird's warm feathers, peeping out to admire the wonders below.

At last they came to the warm countries. The sun shone more brightly and the blue sky seemed twice as high. Blue and green grapes grew all around and there were many groves of oranges and lemons and children played amongst many-colored butterflies.

The swallow flew even further south, and the world beneath them grew even more beautiful. Near a forest on the shores of a blue lake stood an ancient palace of dazzling white marble. Vines twined around lofty pillars and at the tops were clustered many swallows' nests.

"This is my home," the swallow said. "Now, choose for yourself one of the beautiful flowers down below. It will make a perfect home for you."

Among the white marble pillars grew tall, lovely white flowers.

"Wonderful," cried Thumbelina, and the swallow sat her down on the leaves of one of them; and, to Thumbelina's surprise, she saw a little man, no bigger than herself, sitting in the centre of the flower. He was so fine and almost transparent as if he were made of glass, and on his head he wore a crown. On his back were a pair of wings. He was the angel of the flower. In every one of the flowers lived such a tiny angel; and this one was their king.

"How handsome he is," whispered Thumbelina to the swallow. The little king was very frightened of the swallow, for it was a gigantic bird to him. But when he saw Thumbelina he forgot his fear. She was the loveliest creature he had ever seen. He took the crown from his head and placed it on hers.

He asked her name, and if she would be his wife, and then she would be queen of all the flowers. Well, now, here was a far better

husband than slimy Toady, or boring Mr. Mole. Thumbelina smiled at the little king.

"Yes," she said. Out of every flower came a little angel and each brought a present, the best of which was a pair of beautiful wings so she would be able to fly, as they all did, from flower to flower.

And so Thumbelina was married and became Queen of the Flowers. The swallow sat high in his nest and sang for them, but in his heart he was sad. He too loved Thumbelina and hoped never to be parted from her.

"From this day you shall not be called Thumbelina," said the little king, "it is not pretty enough for you. We will call you Maja."

"Farewell, farewell," called the swallow, with a heavy heart, and flew away again, far away back to the North. There he has a nest above the window of a man who tells fairy tales.

"Tweet, tweet," sang the swallow. And the man heard it and wrote down the whole story.